P9-BXZ-919

DEATH IN A HEARTBEAT!

Everything happened faster than a finger snap. But to Josh, who froze to the edge of his seat, it all had a dreamlike slowness to it, as if it were all happening underwater. He remembered the white-faced barkeep leaping under the counter. In the doorway behind the bar, Josh glimpsed a swarthy, heavy-set man with hairy hands—hands clutching a Winchester repeater. Josh never even saw the other man.

Because he was not scooping in or stacking his winnings, Wild Bill's hands were right where he always liked to keep them—thumbs on the seams of his trousers. Even before he had visual confirmation of his targets, Hickok had both guns out. Then he rolled off his chair as the first rifle blasts splintered the wood.

The *Wild Bill* series:

#1: DEAD MAN'S HAND

LEISURE BOOKS  NEW YORK CITY

A LEISURE BOOK®

June 1999

Published by

Dorchester Publishing Co., Inc.
276 Fifth Avenue
New York, NY 10001

If you purchased this book without a cover you should be aware that this book is stolen property. It was reported as "unsold and destroyed" to the publisher and neither the author nor the publisher has received any payment for this "stripped book."

Copyright © 1999 by Dorchester Publishing Co., Inc.

All rights reserved. No part of this book may be reproduced or transmitted in any form or by any electronic or mechanical means, including photocopying, recording or by any information storage and retrieval system, without the written permission of the Publisher, except where permitted by law.

ISBN 0-8439-4529-X

The name "Leisure Books" and the stylized "L" with design are trademarks of Dorchester Publishing Co., Inc.

Printed in the United States of America.

THE KINKAID COUNTY WAR

Chapter One

"Keep your eyes skinned, kid. We're easing in to good ambush country now."

James Butler "Wild Bill" Hickok made this remark as the trail in front of the two horsebackers began to wind through a rocky gorge in central Wyoming's Powder River country. Steep slopes on either side were thick with wild plum and chokecherry bushes.

"What's your plan, Wild Bill?" demanded his eager, fresh-scrubbed companion, nineteen-year-old Joshua Robinson. The young greenhorn from Philadelphia rode his first-ever horse, a gift from Wild Bill. The Sioux-broke *grullo,* or blue mustang, possessed exceptional wind because its nostrils had been slit.

Josh watched Wild Bill's calm, fathomless eyes constantly scan the rocky slopes. He rode a big strawberry roan with a white blaze on its forehead.

"Same plan as always, comfort before business. First we get rooms and a hot bath in Progress City," Bill replied. "Then I plan to wrap my teeth around a beefsteak or two before I scare up a poker game and a bottle of bourbon. After that, we look up a gent named Elmer Kinkaid."

"Is he the gent who hired a Pinkerton man?" Josh pressed.

"To chew it fine," Wild Bill corrected the kid, "it's the Kinkaid County Cattlemen's Association that hired me. But Allan tells me this Elmer fellow is the big bushway hereabouts."

"Allan" was Allan Pinkerton, founder of the American West's first detective agency. Hickok had worked with the Scotsman during the Civil War, gathering reconnaissance for the Army of the Potomac. Now Wild Bill, somewhat reluctantly, had become Pinkerton's best "continental operative." Bill vastly preferred the glory days, when his reputation was worth a lucrative $150-a-month salary for bouncing cowboys around as marshal of Abilene.

But Josh, a newspaperman who was also the official western bureau for the *New York Herald,* knew that Bill's reputation as a dead shot had finally turned against him, as such reputations inevitably do. Now Hickok was the most sought-after human target in America—especially since, while marshal of Abilene, Bill had killed a trouble-seeking Texan named Harlan Lofley. After that, Lofley's wealthy and doting father had placed an open bounty on Hickok's head:

$10,000 in gold double eagles to the man who could prove he killed Hickok.

"Yeah, Bill, but besides just talking to Kinkaid," Josh persisted, "what else you got planned?"

Before he replied, Bill nodded off to their right. Josh watched a fat, shaggy yellow coyote slink off through a gully.

"He's been eating good," Bill said, as if thinking out loud. "I never saw a coyote that fat and sassy. Matter fact, they *all* look that way around here."

Josh assumed Wild Bill was just making another one of his odd observations. The lad admired Hickok greatly. But Wild Bill was a puzzling study. As Josh had written in one of his nationally read columns about Wild Bill: "The man measures corn by his own bushel."

"Bill?" Josh reminded him. "What else you got planned?"

Bill, head still swiveling slowly from side to side as they rode, flashed strong white teeth under a neatly trimmed mustache.

"You're a damn good scribbler, Longfellow. Better than Ned Buntline, and that jasper made me famous, the ink-slinging son of a bitch. But my granddaddy, Otis Hickok, told me writers are the maggots of society."

Josh purpled with anger, but Bill laughed. "Ahh, don't get your pennies in a bunch, kid. I'm just playing the larks with you. Otis *was* a writer. You're a good man to ride the river with. But sometimes your tongue swings way too loose. I don't want the whole damned Kinkaid County to know my next move before I make the damn thing. Y'unnerstan'?''

Actually, Josh did understand, and his anger eased away like a snowflake melting on a river. Some men, Bill was reminding him, came out west to escape injustice; others to escape justice. A man had to be careful, for often it wasn't easy to tell them apart.

They finally cleared the gorge and rode around the shoulder of the last big bluff before the rolling grazeland began.

''There it is, kid,'' Bill announced. ''A grazer's paradise.''

Josh saw lush green grass rolling off toward the eastern horizon, so thick the wind moved through it in waves. Cattle grazed in little, isolated bunches, mostly splotchy Longhorn stock drifted north from Texas ranges. But Josh also saw a few plowed fields with the new ''devil wire'' strung around them to keep cattle off.

Wild Bill sat his saddle, gazing below them while he slid a cheroot and a sulfur match from the pocket of his leather vest. He struck the match with his thumbnail, then fought the wind for a light, barely winning. He watched a farmer, tiny as a grasshopper from here, walk slowly back and forth behind a mule and plow, cutting furrows.

''See those sheep clouds?'' Bill remarked, gazing into the vast blue dome of sky. ''That means rain in twenty-four hours. Place could use it. Don't let that green grass fool you. Spring snowmelt was down this year, way down. One drought, this far west, spells bad trouble for the hoe-men. Means the wheat won't head. This is better cattle country than farmland. But it's the damned government's fault. Preaching all that swamp gas about how 'the rain follows the plow.' "

Josh knew Bill was alluding to the Homestead Act, which allowed new settlers 160-acre land grants at $1.25 per acre, provided they established dwellings and "proved up" the land. The railroad barons and other entrepreneurs were eagerly enticing eastern farmers farther and farther west to establish new communities along the railroad lines. But this reckless expansionism was pitting the homesteaders against the cattle kings, and something had to give.

"Gee up, Fire-away!" Bill pressured the roan with his knees, and the two riders moved down onto the open ranges. Though it was still late April, the afternoon was brittle with hot sun. But Josh knew that, come dawn, there would be a thin powdering of frost on the grass.

The trail, two thin ruts established by the Overland coach, dipped between two broad knolls covered with jackpine. Abruptly, a dead Longhorn steer cropped into view ahead of them, lying perhaps ten yards off the trail.

Wild Bill reined in, swung down, and handed his reins to Josh. Walking a bit stiff-legged from an old leg wound, Bill crossed to the bloated carcass and knelt to examine it.

"Poisoned," Bill finally announced. "With strychnine, just like Pinkerton said. You can tell by how the tongue twisted and turned blue."

Josh wrinkled his face in disgust at the putrid stench. The corpse was crawling with bluebottle flies. And it wasn't the only dead Longhorn they spotted—piles of bleaching bones dotted the area as they rode on east toward Progress City.

More and more barbed wire—"bobwire" to the cowboys—showed up as they rode into the heart of Kinkaid County. In many places, the wind had piled Russian thistles against the fences. Toward sundown, the riders reached a spot where an old plank bridge crossed a clear, sand-bottomed creek.

"If we keep on," Bill said, consulting an Army map Pinkerton had given him, "we won't likely make Progress City until midnight or so. Might as well pitch camp right here for the night, ride in by daylight. I don't like to kick hotel clerks awake."

Josh could hear the disappointment in Bill's voice. The man was indifferent to human company but not to human comforts, particularly poker and his beloved Old Taylor bourbon. Nor was he one to ignore a high-toned woman, if one was available.

The two riders loosed their cinches and pulled their saddles, then dropped their bits and bridles before tethering the horses in good graze near the creek. Following Bill's example, Josh used handfuls of dry grass to rub down his sweaty mustang. Both animals were also curried and checked for saddle galls before the men turned to their own needs.

Josh watched Wild Bill carefully study the terrain around them in the gathering darkness.

"We'll build a fire," he decided. "But we'll keep

it in a pit. Pinkerton warned me before we rode out of Denver, somebody will likely be watching for us. Before you turn in, make sure that gun I gave you is loaded and ready to hand.''

Josh, busy crumbling bark kindling into a fresh-scooped pit, watched Bill carefully select a cottonwood with a five-foot bole, then sit down with his back to it. Josh had never known a man more constantly aware of his surroundings—or a man with greater need to *stay* aware.

As usual, Bill relaxed and tended to his weapons while Josh took care of the camp details.

''You know, Longfellow,'' Bill remarked, rolling out the cylinder on one of his pearl-gripped Colt Peacemakers and checking the loads, ''Bill Hickok is usually a one-man outfit. I didn't think much, at first, about your idea to sidekick with me for a while. But I have to admit it, you're a handy man to have along. Handy as a pocket in a shirt, matter fact. Good cook, too. Say, knock us up some grub, wouldja? You cook damn fine beans, kid.''

Josh was plenty proud to actually be riding shotgun with the most famous gunman in the West. But he couldn't help wondering sometimes if Bill didn't tolerate him just to get a free cook and manservant.

Darkness settled over them like a black velvet cloak. The hum of cicadas rose and fell in a sweet, harmonic cadence. A fish jumped in the nearby creek.

''Put a trotline out before you turn in,'' Bill suggested. ''We'll have fresh bass for breakfast.''

Josh separated the halves of his bull's-eye canteen,

turning it into two metal dishes. He began spooning hot pinto beans into them. Both men ate in silence for a few minutes.

"Wild Bill?"

"Mmm?"

Bill finished his first helping of beans and pushed back from the glow of the firepit. Josh could barely make him out against the cottonwood, picking his teeth with a twig. Josh started spooning more beans into Bill's dish.

"All this cattle poisoning—you think it'll get rough for us?"

"Kid, it can get rough in cattle country. Rough as boar bristles. Especially in the cowtowns like Abilene and Hays City on a Saturday night. But say? If you ever spent some time in the mining camps of the Black Hills, you'd call everything else a Sunday stroll. We may never have to bust a cap on this job. These cowmen and farmers, why, they're tough and stubborn, sure. But they're no shootists. I'd wager that—"

The sudden, nearby detonation of a rifle cartridge instantly closed Josh's throat. The dish he had just handed to Wild Bill flew from Hickok's hands, hot beans spattering both men.

Bill reacted before Josh could even get his heart started again. He leaped forward, tackled Josh, and rolled hard with him, flinging him into a natural sink for cover.

"Cover down, kid, and stay there!"

There was just enough buttery moonlight for Josh

to see what happened next. Wild Bill utterly amazed him by quickly rolling out into the open. The man came up on his heels, fanning the hammer of one of his Colts.

Because Bill couldn't exactly pinpoint the dry-gulcher, he opted for overwhelming firepower. Josh watched him tuck and roll, tuck and roll, firing again each time he came up from the ground. Red fire streaked from his barrels. He emptied both guns, twelve rapid shots in a sweeping arc.

Cartridges clinked as they fell against rocks. Josh whiffed the acrid stink of spent cordite. When Bill's guns fell silent, Josh heard distant cursing, then a horse's hooves pounding out across the flats.

"You okay, kid?"

Josh swallowed the stone in his throat. "I think so. See anything, Bill?"

"All I spotted was the blue barrel of a Winchester."

Wild Bill slapped dust from his trousers and retrieved his flat-brimmed black hat. Before he did anything else, he thumbed cartridges into his empty revolvers.

"I started to say," Bill commented sarcastically, "I'd wager this job will be easier than rolling off a log. But I forgot how sly Pinkerton is. That old skinflint has sent us up Salt River once again, kid. From here on out, keep your nose to the wind. I see now that lead *will* fly."

Chapter Two

A fancy fringed surrey, with fresh blacking on the dashboard and a new whip in the socket, eased to a stop in the narrow alley behind the Progress City Land Registrar's Office. The driver wrapped the reins around the brake handle and leaped athletically to the ground.

Johnny Kinkaid hustled around to the passenger's side and handed down a young woman encumbered by hoop skirts and a huge silk bustle. She wore widow's black, although the period for a veil and gloves was long past.

"Won't be but a few minutes in here, Dottie," Johnny assured her. "Then I'll drive you back to your place."

The woman was pretty, but had a coarse, roadhouse manner about her. "Could you maybe stay out to my place a bit?'' Dottie suggested, searching to make eye contact with him. ''Like you done last time? Maybe have a look at that busted pump? It gets . . . difficult for a lady that's lost her man in this godforsaken wilderness. I mean . . . there's so many things that go ignored when a woman's by herself, if you take my meaning?''

''I take it,'' Johnny muttered, biting off the rest of his sarcastic thought. Firmly pressuring her by one elbow, he led her toward the raw plank door at the front of the land office. ''We'll see, hon. Business before pleasure.''

The scornful twist of Kinkaid's mouth was a family trait. He was about twenty-one, good-looking and well aware of it, with cold eyes as gray as morning frost. He wore a big, Cavalry-issue Smith & Wesson pistol, holster tied low on his right thigh.

Dottie scowled at his brusque manner. The pig! Nothing came before a Kinkaid man's pleasure, and they'd tell any lie to bed a woman. But she could feel the weight of new Liberty Eagles clinking in her drawstring purse. So as they entered the cramped cubbyhole of the land office, Dottie dutifully tried to look sad and grieving.

''Mornin', Sam!'' Johnny called out to an anemic little clerk wearing sleeve garters and a green eyeshade. He was swatting at flies behind a scarred deal counter. ''Stir your stumps, buddy! We got another title transfer. Section 977. It's a quarter-section down on Turk's Creek.''

''You betcha, Johnny! G'day, Mrs. McGratten.''

Sam Watson tossed his feather flyswatter aside and began searching in his file drawers. They held titles, and records-of-claim for titles, representing thousands of sections of land in vast Kinkaid and Converse Counties. Good land sold for next to nothing under the Homestead Act.

"Here we go," Sam said, pulling a title out and studying it through thick bifocals. "Section 977. Will that be transferred into Elmer's name, Johnny, or yours?" Sam asked in his best ingratiating manner.

"Mine," Johnny said. "And just in case your trail should cross my old man's, which ain't likely with him crippled up like he is—you keep all this dark from him, y'hear?"

A gold coin bounced off the counter and was whisked into Sam's fob pocket before it could bounce twice.

"You betcha, Johnny. Just sign here in your husband's place, Mrs. McGratten, may Corporal McGratten rest in peace."

"An American hero," Dottie agreed piously, though in fact her man had died of syphilis while on an extended scout in Sioux country. It had been reported as a combat death to spare the frontier Army's already tarnished image.

Dottie scrawled her name with a steel nib Sam dipped in a pot of ink for her.

"Heard of any new soldier's widows?" Johnny asked the clerk bluntly while Dottie pretended deafness.

"Not yet, but I'm watching the *Police Gazette,*"

Sam assured Kinkaid. "It lists every soldier killed, by location, and names his immediate family."

"Good man." Johnny nodded, affixing his own signature to the deed as the new owner of Government Section 977. "Don't forget, Sam. One gold shiner for every name."

For the past year or so, Johnny Kinkaid had secretly been hiring soldier's widows to register land filings. He was usually able to buy the titles within months of filing—sometimes even weeks. By federal law, the service period of a soldier killed on duty was subtracted from his widow's required period of residence upon a homestead.

Furthermore, widows were not required to "prove up" or improve the land in any way. Nor did they have to build a dwelling or even occupy the land before they transferred title.

"You know, Johnny," Sam said timidly, clearing his throat, "Hansen and the rest of the hoe-men are tryin' to go to law over in Casper. They want all unoccupied filings subject to contest. Most especial, those around Bar Nunn, Mills, and Evansville that border on Turk's Creek."

Johnny snorted like a master stallion. "I hear the damned is wantin' ice water in hell, too, Sammy. Don't fret. *Let* 'em go to law. Judges like shiners, too. 'Sides that, we ain't breaking no laws."

Johnny led Dottie outside. Across the sun-drenched ruts of the town's only street, a big, rawboned Swede was gingerly loading a roll of barbed wire into a buckboard. He wore whipcord trousers, gone through at the knees. One broken boot was wrapped tight with burlap to reinforce it.

"Hey, Hansen!" Kinkaid shouted when he spotted him. "Know what? Bobwire is easier to cut than to string!"

"Yah, for a fact! And know what else? It's easier to kill a man than to argue with him," Dave Hansen shot back.

"That a threat?"

"Yah, you're goldang right it is, Kinkaid. I catch you at my wire, you unchristian sot, I blow your belly open with buckshot!"

Johnny's mouth twisted in contempt. "You filthy seed-stickers are all alike. Poor as Job's turkey, alla yous. But you got plenty of mouth. Why'n't you quit hot-jawing your betters and strap on a short iron, big man?"

"I may be poor, Kinkaid, but there's no shadow on my name. A man can be proud of that."

Johnny dropped Dottie's arm and took two steps out into the street. His right hand rested on the metal backstrap of his Smith & Wesson. "What's your drift, Hansen?"

Dave backed away from his first reply, not sure how far to push the younger Kinkaid. Elmer's boy was not exactly known as a frontier bully who shot unarmed men. But he was reckless and hotheaded. And he derived great pleasure from humbling a foe before killing him, to make him realize he'd been beaten by a better man.

"Go to hell, Johnny. I don't spit when a Kinkaid says hawk."

The big Swede turned his back. Kinkaid's sneer deepened. "The time's coming, Hansen. You'll fight or show yellow, you soft-mouthed son of a bitch."

Johnny turned to take Widow McGratten's elbow again. Abruptly, he made eye contact with a well-dressed, middle-aged man who'd just emerged from the Medicine Bow Hotel across the street. The man was clearly "East Coast capital" and not a local. He wore a dark twill suit and a neat bowler hat, and carried a slender walking stick tipped with an ivory knob.

Johnny nodded once before he turned away and guided Dottie toward the surrey waiting in the alley. The man watched him for a moment. Then he smiled and headed down the street toward the Western Union office.

"They've had nothing but fodder for almost a week now," Wild Bill told a half-wit-looking kid. "Feed 'em up good on corn and oats, wouldja?"

The hostler nodded absently, for Josh could see that he was watching Bill's roan enjoy a good roll in the hoof-packed yard of the livery stable. "Yessir. Mister, that's a *fine* horse. Best I've seen in a spell now. And that little blue Indian cayuse ain't no slouch neither, I'd wager."

"And you'd win," Bill assured him, realizing the kid was smarter than he looked. "Both those horses can gallop from hell to breakfast. Son, if it's good weather tonight, don't stall either animal. Turn 'em out into the corral."

"Yessir."

Bill threw a tired arm around Josh's shoulders. The older man's handsome face was beard-smudged and gray with trail dust. The Hickok nobody ever photographed, Josh realized.

"C'mon, Longfellow," Wild Bill said. "Let's stow our rigs, then get the lay of this place."

Both men carried their saddles into the big barn and threw them onto saddle racks in the tack room. They hung their bridles on nails, then headed back out into the rutted street.

Unlike many western towns Josh had seen so far, Progress City had plenty of trees, and they were budding into leaf. The livery stood at the far western edge of town. This side of the street included a bank, a blacksmith's forge, a Western Union office, a saloon, and the land office at the opposite edge of town. The far side of the single, straight street included a general store, the sheriff's office and jailhouse, a hardware, a barber's shop, and a two-story frame hotel with a high false front.

"I don't see a separate wash-house," Bill told the kid. "Prob'ly the hotel sells hot baths."

As they strolled, Josh marveled again at Hickok's smooth manner. The man looked relaxed and easy. But by now Josh had learned that Hickok's hair-trigger alertness never let the slightest detail slip by.

Within seconds, for example, Bill had made a mental map of the entire street and its denizens: the usual crew of town loafers, track hands, reservation bucks, women in calico sun-bonnets, and assorted hard tails. This last group was the only one Bill paid close attention to—the dirty men with lidded eyes and notched guns, holding up the buildings with their hips while they menaced every passerby.

"Those're the easy-money lemmings," Bill told Josh in a low tone. "Every town's got 'em. That's it, Junior, just keep smiling wide at 'em. You look sweet as a scrubbed angel, Longfellow."

By now Josh had learned to ignore Bill's insulting patter. It was all a distraction. Hickok was nervously dreading being recognized. He was fastidious about his clothing, and now wore a long gray duster to protect his suit. But it also hid his distinctive pearl-gripped Colts. So far, no one had recognized Wild Bill and run forward to ask if he could touch him for luck—or to take a shot at him.

But Josh knew that Bill feared more than one kind of ambush. At one point, a bead of nervous sweat trickled out of Wild Bill's hairline. Hickok asked in a tense voice, "You don't see her, do you, kid?"

With effort, Josh stifled a grin. "Her" was Martha Jane Burke—better known in frontier circles as Calamity Jane. It was widely known the woman had a serious itch, and she was convinced that only Wild Bill Hickok could scratch it.

"Nothing so far," Josh replied.

"She'll show," Bill muttered. "Sure as cats fighting."

The Medicine Bow Hotel was typical of a dozen

such establishments Josh had stayed in since throwing in with Wild Bill. The lobby was dominated by a rusted stove set on brick legs, and the rough floor of foot-wide, unsanded boards showed huge cracks between them. Tin lamp reflectors lined the narrow hallways, and the legs of all the beds had been set in bowls of kerosene to keep off the bedbugs.

A clerk in a high, bright-glazed paper collar handed both guests a key and spun the register around so they could sign in. ''Steam boiler out back, gents, all the hot water you'll need. Get your towels and soap from the little Chinee boy, Mr. . . . *Hickok!*''

The clerk's eyes widened when he saw the register. Josh knew that Wild Bill never bothered to use an alias. Instead, Hickok flipped a gold piece onto the counter.

''Would it be such a problem,'' Bill said to the clerk in a low tone, ''if the register says we're in rooms that're actually empty?''

The clerk never batted an eye. Without a word he wrote ''Room 212'' after Bill's name, ''Room 212'' after Josh's. In fact, both men were assigned to adjacent rooms on the first floor.

The clerk slid the gold back to Wild Bill. ''Keep your money, Bill. I owe you my life. The name is Rault—Jed Rault. I was with the First Illinois Rifles under General Hoffman. Your report on the Rebels' secret artillery nests at Nashville came through *just* in the nick of time. Saved my division from a massacre. You were the best scout and spy the Union put in the field.''

Bill offered his hand, and the two Civil War vets gave each other a hearty grip.

The clerk glanced around discreetly before adding, "I can guess why you're here, Bill. Just take care, both of you. It ain't just cattle dying early around here."

"Wild Bill Hickok, as I live and breathe!"

The suave baritone voice came from behind them, startling both new arrivals. Josh saw Bill go rigid as a poker. He had violated one of his sacred rules—somehow, he had let a man slip into the room unobserved.

Bill turned slowly around. A well-dressed, courteously smiling gentleman holding a slender walking stick gave both men a slight bow.

"Wild Bill Hickok!" he repeated. "What an extraordinary pleasure. Sir, your reputation as a shootist is *almost* matched by your reputation as a poker aficionado. My name is Jarvis Blackford, a drummer by trade. Would you perhaps be interested in a game of chance later this evening?"

Bill flashed a grin through the dusty patina on his face. *This* kind of challenge he relished. "Is Paris a city? I'll look for you in the lounge, Mr. Blackford."

Chapter Three

The next morning, Bill got directions from Jed Rault, the hotel clerk. Then Bill and Josh made the five-mile ride out to Elmer Kinkaid's Rocking K spread.

"That Mr. Blackford fella," Josh remarked as their mounts trotted along a good road established by the local short-line stage. "Nice enough gent, but he ain't much of a hand at poker, is he? Man alive! He musta lost a hundred dollars to you last night."

"One hundred and seven dollars, to be exact."

Even as he replied, Bill monitored the sprawling country to both sides of the trail. They were safe from ambush here in the open grass flats. But Josh and Bill had both seen plenty of reminders that a war was heating up hereabouts. They had spotted more dead and bloated cattle, obviously poisoned, as well as cut fences and trampled crops.

"If I was that bad at cards," Josh observed, "I'd take up dominoes or checkers."

"Blackford is an excellent cardplayer," Bill said quietly, watching a wedge of geese head north. "Better than Bill Hickok. But he cheated."

"Cheated!" Josh's jaw dropped in astonishment. "But he lost!"

Bill nodded. His face, smooth-shaven now, was half in shadow under the black brim of his hat.

"My point exactly, Longfellow. He cheated *himself* so I would win. Once, he even discarded a wild card."

"But why?" Josh demanded. The young reporter was due to file a story soon by telegraphic dispatch. And he sniffed a compelling mystery here.

"That's a good question, kid. Nobody gives you something for nothing except your mother. And Jarvis Blackford is not the motherly type."

Josh hated it when Bill acted so damned cryptic. But despite a barrage of questions, Bill maintained silence for the rest of the trip.

They topped the summit of a long, low ridge and spotted the Rocking K below them in a grassy hollow fed by a big creek. A sprawling one-story ranch house built of fieldstone was surrounded by weathered-plank outbuildings and several pole corrals.

Punchers were busy in a big pasture behind the house, branding and dehorning yearling steers. No one paid much attention as the two riders entered the main yard and hobbled their mounts at a long stone watering trough.

Bill knuckled the front door frame. A moment later, Josh gaped in astonishment at the beauty who answered. The young woman wore a floral-print dress that swelled generously at the bosom. Her thick, coffee-colored hair was pulled into a chignon at the nape of her neck. Her cheeks, Josh noted with wide-eyed approval, glowed like fall apples. She held two paper bags.

"Well," she greeted them uncertainly, eyes darting between both men to take their measure. "Our maid said two riders were coming into the yard. Since it's close to dinnertime, I assumed you'd be out-of-work cowboys looking for a bite to eat. But neither of you gentlemen appears very destitute."

Josh understood the bags now. It was the custom, in cattle country, for the wealthiest ranchers to feed local, out-of-work cowboys. Bill took one of the bags, opened it, saw a sandwich, an apple, and a doughnut. He removed the apple, handed the bag back, and began shining the apple on his vest while he frankly appraised the beauty.

"I suddenly have an appetite," Bill said, greeting her. "This apple looks *tempting*. Miss . . . ?"

"Kinkaid. Nell Kinkaid. But a man who looks like *you* can call me Eve."

Still watching her, his bottomless blue eyes twinkling, Bill bit deeply into the fresh, sweet, juicy fruit.

"Kid," he informed Josh between chews, "on the frontier, people generally fall into two societies. They're either dancers or they've got Methodist feet. I'd wager Nell here is one of the dancers."

"Sir, I see you fancy yourself quite the expert on women," Nell shot back. "Do you know us from theory or experience?"

"Don't mind my daughter, Mr. Hickok," came a tobacco-roughened voice from behind Nell. "That girl's just like her ma was, may she rest in peace. Pretty as four aces and brash as a government mule. Come in, Wild Bill, come in, I've been expecting you since Pinkerton sent a telegram. This is a great honor."

Only now realizing who the handsome man in the duster was, Nell flushed and stepped aside to let the visitors in. Josh saw an old man in a wheelchair behind her.

"I'm Elmer Kinkaid," he announced. "Stove up, but still feisty. Welcome to the Rocking K spread, gents. Jenny!" he called to a young maid in a mob-cap. "Serve us coffee in the front parlor."

Bill quickly introduced Josh. The young *New York Herald* reporter already knew that old man Kinkaid had been permanently crippled in a toss from his horse six years earlier. Though it left him confined to a wheelchair, he still ran the Kinkaid cattle empire with the same iron will and fist.

"Sorry my boy Johnny couldn't be here," Elmer said. "He's supervising the branding of the yearlings. The ones that ain't been poisoned, that is," Kinkaid added bitterly. "If *you* can't get to the bottom of all this, Bill, I'm selling out, and to hell with raising beeves."

By now they had all settled in a comfortable parlor

featuring red plush furniture with a fancy knotted fringe. Josh had been unable to take his eyes off Nell, but she, in turn, had eyes only for Wild Bill. Josh felt a familiar sting of jealousy. Playing sidekick to a living legend—especially one noted for good looks—was hell on a man's love life.

"Even a blind man can see what's going on around Kinkaid County," Bill told the old patriarch. "Trouble is, a man can't judge only by appearances. Especially a stranger to these parts. So you tell me how *you* see it."

The weathered grooves of his face deepened when Elmer frowned. He twisted a finger into his soup-strainer mustache, mulling Bill's question. Josh noticed that the old man had been working at a little table, carving a new gunstock from a block of walnut. Elmer's hands were crippled up from a life of hard labor, but he still did good work with them.

"This area is settling up," Kinkaid finally replied. "Nothing wrong with that. Hell, I welcome newcomers. *I* was new here once, myself, and didn't have a pot to spit in. But these new settlers we get now? Hell, half of 'em are goddamn Pops," Elmer added bitterly, meaning Populists. "They hate the rich man on principle. And they've got 'em a mouthpiece name o' Dave Hansen. A Swedish sodbuster who's got one hell of an ax to grind. And mister, he means to grind it till the wheel breaks."

"So you figure this Hansen is the ringleader behind the poisonings?"

"I figure it, I know it, but damn my eyes if I can

prove it. Especially from this damned chair."

"What about the sheriff in Progress City?" Bill asked. "He honest?"

Elmer snorted. "Waldo is middling honest, all right. Trouble is, he ain't got the mentality for the job. Matter of fact, he ain't got the brains God gave a pissant."

Elmer pulled open the top drawer of his little worktable. He removed a one-ounce bottle of white powder.

"This is strychnine, Mr. Hickok. A little pinch of this cheap white powder will kill most any varmint. Especially since the sheepmen moved in, we got a real problem hereabouts with coyotes and gray wolves. Trouble is, everybody hereabouts has strychnine on hand. And it kills cattle, too."

"Do you have any hard evidence," Bill asked, "that Hansen's poisoning cattle?"

"Evidence? Hell no! That's why there ain't no end to the damned lawing hereabouts. Hansen's been spotted near the worst poisoning sites. Trouble is, he's got him a good excuse for being spotted all over. See, he locates new settlers for a small fee. Helps them find the government corners on their land."

Bill nodded. The section corners of each land-grant plot were marked with four small holes, often difficult to find without help from locals.

"This Dave Hansen," Bill pressed. "Is he the killing kind? I ask because Josh and I were dry-gulched outside of Progress City."

Josh watched Elmer give that one some thought,

again twisting a finger into his shaggy mustache. "I can't say, Wild Bill. I despise the man, but I'm not so sure Hansen is a cold-blooded killer. But there's others around here—other hoe-men, I mean—that are lower than a snake's belly."

"Maybe a few low cattlemen, too?" Bill prodded.

Kinkaid's white eyebrows met in a frown. "The hell's that mean? *We* hired you, Hickok. Don't crap where you eat."

Bill let it go for now. Before he could ask any more questions, a puncher in dusty work clothes appeared at one of the open windows and politely requested to speak with the boss.

"Keep Mr. Hickok entertained, Nell," Elmer said before he wheeled his chair across to the window. "But watch him. I hear he's quite the lady's man."

After the old man was out of earshot, Josh saw Nell catch Bill's eye. "*I'll* be safe with you, won't I, Mr. Hickok? After all, you only squire wealthy and famous women, isn't that right? Actresses, singers, countesses, and the like? Not a common ranch girl like me."

"Actually," Bill replied easily, "quality is all I look for—in a horse *or* a woman."

"And just how does one determine quality, Mr. Hickok?"

"Well, in the case of a horse, Miss Kinkaid," Bill said, his voice thick with innuendo, "one ride is generally sufficient."

Josh watched Nell blush to her earlobes. She hadn't meant to get in this deep. Trapped now, she dug herself in even deeper. "One ride? But what if you're bucked off?"

Bill nodded, thoroughly enjoying himself now. "Even better. I like spirit . . . in a horse."

Josh was starting to blush, himself, when Elmer finished his discussion and rolled back to join the others. While he spoke with Nell, Bill had been eyeing a long shelf on the back wall. It was heavy with trophy cups, all awarded for superior marksmanship. Elmer saw Bill studying the shelf.

"My boy's handiwork," Elmer said scornfully. "Johhny's a gun-slick and proud of it. Practices drawing and shooting every day, has since he was twelve. Boy's won him over a dozen shooting matches. It's hogwash! A cattleman don't even need a short gun 'cept to kill snakes 'n' such."

Bill shrugged. "Snakes come in many sizes, Mr. Kinkaid."

Bill rose and Josh followed suit. " 'Preciate your time," Wild Bill told Elmer. "I'll speak with Hansen and have a good look around, see which way the wind sets. I'll get back with you, Mr. Kinkaid."

"Pleasure meeting you, Wild Bill. Just a warning: You've been jumped once already, and it'll happen again. There's plenty hereabouts who know about the open reward on your hide. You cover your ampersand."

"Yes," echoed Nell Kinkaid as she escorted both men to the door. She lowered her voice so Elmer couldn't hear when she added, "Now that I've tempted you with an apple, Mr. Hickok, it would be a shame if you don't return to visit Eve in her garden.''

Bill started to reply, but Nell only smiled mysteriously before closing the door in his face.

Chapter Four

Late in the afternoon, the three of them met in an isolated line shack at the extreme northern boundary of the Rocking K property: Johnny Kinkaid, Jarvis Blackford, and Barry Tate, foreman of the Rocking K.

"Confrontation is *not* the way," Blackford insisted in his city-cultured voice. "Not with Hickok. Have you forgotten what he did to the McCanles gang in Kansas? Or that he single-handedly pacified Hays City—a wide-open cowtown with twenty-two saloons? Hickok has more kills than John Wesley Hardin. At least forty."

"Jarvis may have struck a lode," Tate chimed in. The foreman was around thirty, a blunt-jawed, hawk-nosed man with thick red burnsides. "Me and some of the boys gave Hickok a little welcome outside of town. That bastard tossed a mineful of lead back at us!"

Johnny's expressive mouth twisted in scorn. "An old woman can toss lead! How much of it scored any hits, huh? Fear the man, not the dime novels. Hickok always keeps a newspaper reporter in his hip pocket. *That's* how come men get snow in their boots around him."

Blackford, neatly turned out in a three-piece suit, shook his head. "Johnny, you've got enough guts to fill a smokehouse. And I, for one, think you might even be faster on the draw than Hickok. But you're a hothead. Wild Bill is also *wily* Bill. He hasn't just got speed and skill on his side. The man also has excellent instincts and nerves of Toledo steel. He shoots first and he asks questions later."

Johnny scowled, but as usual he showed some deference to the older man. Jarvis Blackford might be a bit of a dandy, but then so was Wild Bill Hickok. Jarvis didn't make it to the top in the tough railroad business by being weak *or* stupid.

"If he's got such 'excellent instincts,' " Johnny suggested, "then ain't you paring the cheese mighty close to the rind, Jarvis? I mean, becoming the man's poker buddy? Ain't you worried he'll find out you're a big nabob with the Burlington instead of just some hardware drummer?"

The dilapidated line shack had a rammed-earth floor with an old Franklin stove hunkering in the middle of the only room. A skunk-oil lamp with a rag wick and the packing crate it sat upon were the only furnishings besides a crude shakedown bunk in the back corner.

Jarvis, busy clearing the stem of his fancy rosewood pipe, scoffed at Johnny's suggestion. "Nonsense, stout lad. I really *was* a hardware drummer at one time. I know the business. Besides, no one else in town but you two know my real position. So long as we three make sure to meet secretly, the risk is acceptable. Fortune favors the bold, my friend."

"Besides," Tate added, "this way we can know, at least sometimes, exactly where Hickok will be. Like tonight—Hickok's playing five-card with Jarvis at the hotel starting around eight o'clock. That leaves the coast clear for us to visit Hansen."

"My point exactly." Blackford nodded, testing the draw on his pipe. "Johnny, *your* passion is practicing with your pistols. Hickok's is cards. Once that man is riding a streak, he'd skip his own mother's funeral. In fact, gambling is his one weakness—that and his fondness for pretty women. Hickok told a reporter he'll likely *die* at a poker table."

"Now, that ain't a bad idea," Johnny said. "Pop the son of a bitch while he's counting his winnings."

"My point," Jarvis insisted, "is that the more I convince him he's on a streak, the less likely he'll be to leave that hotel nights."

A frown had divided Tate's bluff face at the allusion to Hickok's "fondness for pretty women." The foreman had been worried for hours about that skirt-chasing bastard being in the same room with Nell Kinkaid. She was too pert to resist. And Barry was bound and determined to slap *his* brand on her first.

"Well, I ain't one to take the long way around a

barn,'' Johnny said. ''But you've made a good offer, Mr. Blackford. And you must know what you're talking about or you wouldn't be in a position to *make* that offer. So we'll play it by your rules for now.''

''Good man. For right now, it's best to keep up the appearance that we've got a classic war between the farmers and the ranchers, with the farmers egging it on the worst. That keeps the local law effectively out of it. Sheriff Waldo is supposedly neutral. But he knows it's cattle revenues that pay county salaries, not foreclosed mortgages on dried-up cornfields.''

''There'll be more blood soon,'' Johnny warned. ''Hansen is pushing—pushing hard since Barry shot that German preacher out on Grass Creek. We damn near hugged yesterday in town.''

Jarvis nodded, cheeks caving in as he drew at his pipe. ''Blood usually comes with a war.''

''And Hickok's blood,'' Barry reminded them, ''is redeemable for ten thousand dollars. I made sure that every nickel-chaser in the territory knows he's here. It'll get warm for Mr. Hickok. Mighty damn warm.''

''Dogs!''

Martha ''Calamity Jane'' Burke cursed and drew back on the reins as she cleared a stand of ponderosa pine and spotted three horses tethered in front of the shack.

''Dogs!'' she repeated in a grating voice like pebbles caught in a sluice gate. ''Sun going low and no supper. Tarnal blazes!''

Jane was stout and strong, with a homely, careworn face. She wore her greasy hair tied into a heavy knot that dangled under an immaculate gray Stetson—the only clean item she wore besides the Volcanic pistol tucked into a bright red sash around her waist. She drove a dilapidated buckboard with gaudily painted sideboards advertising DOYLE'S HOP BITTERS: "THE INVALID'S FRIEND AND HOPE."

Doyle's was one of the most popular patent medicines in the country. As a curative it was worthless. But its heavy dose of alcohol left the patient too drunk to care. Jane always drank what she couldn't sell—and often drank what she *should* have sold.

From a long habit of solitude, Calamity Jane always talked to her team of swaybacked bays as if they were old friends.

"I knew that line shack wouldn't stay deserted forever," she complained to them now. "But I figured another couple weeks before any punchers moved in."

Jane had been staying in the shack since arriving in Kinkaid County two days earlier. She knew such line shacks were occupied only after the cattle had been driven farther from the grass-scarce winter ranges, up here into the high-country summer pastures. She had left the shack for an hour or so to check on her rabbit snares. Now she was undecided what to do—wait here a spell, or go and pitch a camp somewhere before sunset?

"Them ain't all cow ponies," Calamity Jane told

her team, noticing the fancy, silver-trimmed Mexican saddle on that big claybank. The other two horses definitely belonged to cow nurses. Jane could tell this from the saddles—their high pommels and narrow cantles, designed to accommodate slim-hipped cowboys. But that third horse belonged to an outsider.

"Now, ain't that uncommon queer?" Jane asked her team. "Or is it? Seems as how Bill Hickok's arrival in a territory always draws outsiders like flies to syrup."

And concerning flies, Jane had learned a motto from Bill, *the* love of her young life: Kill one, kill a thousand.

Jane had lost her heart to Wild Bill Hickok exactly four years earlier, in the spring of 1868, when she first laid eyes on the garish cover of Ned Buntline's sensational *Wild Bill, Indian Fighter*. But that handsome, wild-eyed Army scout depicted on the cover paled before the beauty and savage masculinity of the real man himself.

A lovestruck Jane had visited a famous palm reader in Old El Paso. The old *abuela* read Jane's deep-seamed palm for almost an hour, declaring that her destiny was meant to converge with that of "*un hombre famoso, guapo, y muy, muy peligroso*"—a famous, handsome, and very, very dangerous man.

That description fit Bill Hickok like a second skin. And from that day forth, Jane had found her purpose in life: to go where Bill went, to protect him with her own life, if need be. That man meant more to Jane than the breath in her nostrils.

There was a minor problem, of course. Bill hadn't realized—yet—that the two of them were separate halves of one unified destiny. But that day was coming, Jane's love line promised it.

In the meantime, she thought as she studied those three horses, she had to keep her reckless man alive.

"You sons of bitches can rob a bank or heist a stage," Jane muttered. "Steal a damned steamboat, for aught I care. But you draw down on Bill Hickok, you filthy pond scum, and you best pray *he* kills you before I do."

Dave Hansen batched in an old sod dugout located near Turk's Creek. After getting directions from Elmer Kinkaid, Wild Bill and Josh set out across the rolling grass flats. They took their time, for Bill was interested in surveying the area and making a mental map of the terrain.

They were further delayed when a sudden thunderstorm boiled up. Gray sheets of driving rain forced them to take shelter under a traprock shelf. The sudden deluge left patches of mud as thick and sloppy as gumbo. As the two riders resumed their trek, flashes of heat lightning illuminated the darkening landscape. Now and then a mighty clap of thunder rocked the ground.

Turk's Creek, actually a small river in spring, was only one of several major water sources in Kinkaid County. It was also the area most settled by farmers. As the sun set, Wild Bill and Josh followed the creek's meandering course for several miles. And now the *other* destructive side of the Kinkaid County War was evident.

"Fences down and crops ripped right from the ground," Bill told Josh. He dismounted and pointed to a fence post. "Look—somebody deliberately pulled all the staples out and *took* them so it would be harder to put the fences back up. And look there—"

The sudden crack of a rifle shot split the evening silence with commanding authority. Josh barely had time to tense before Wild Bill had shoved him face-first into the mud.

Another shot, a third, sent columns of muddy water into the air only inches from Josh's head.

"Hansen!" Bill roared out, raising his long yellow curls out of the mud soup. "Stand down, you damned fool! We're *not* night riders! My name is Bill Hickok, and I've come to talk to you!"

"Hickok? Yah, shoor! And *my* name is Queen Victoria!"

"I can believe that, you dumb Swede. *She's* a trigger-happy hothead, too!"

"I don't know your voice, mister, so I'll hold my fire while you two show yourselves. But by God, don't get cute on me! Hands up high. Yah, that's it."

Despite their predicament, Josh grinned at the disgusted look on Bill's face as he slapped the muck off his clothing. The fastidious Hickok would rather face a blazing six-gun than get his wardrobe messy.

Josh saw their captor coming toward them across

the moon-bleached landscape, a long Henry rifle trained on them. Dave Hansen was a big, barrel-chested man—"strong as a sheepman's socks," as a local saying went. But he also had tired eyes and a quick, nervous manner that irritated Josh. He was clearly a high-strung and excitable man—the wrong type to thrive out west.

"By grab, you *are* Bill Hickok!" the farmer said, lowering the muzzle of his Henry. "I don't know why you're on my property, Bill, but I know you wouldn't come to harm a dirt-poor farmer. So welcome."

Bill quickly explained that Pinkerton had sent him to investigate the troubles in Kinkaid County. He didn't mention, however, that the cattlemen were paying him.

"I already talked to Elmer Kinkaid," Bill concluded. "He says you and the farmers are the problem, not the cattlemen. Says you're poisoning his cattle."

"The farmers, my sweet aunt!" Hansen exploded. "Why, it's Tammany politics in the short-grass country! When the cowmen first started this war, I had half a mind to tie the cow to the endgate and just move on. But common troubles will knit men. Now, by the living God, us hoe-men mean to give as good as we get."

"You deny poisoning any cattle?" Bill pressed.

"Yah, shoor, you goddamn right I deny it! And my cousin Ned Droullard didn't kill no cows neither. He was a Lutheran preacher, had a little farm out on

Grass Creek. We found him dead of colic, Bill. *Lead* colic.''

''So who *is* killing the beeves?'' Wild Bill demanded.

''I'll be damned if *I* care, Bill! Let 'em die! All I know is, eastern capital is the goddamn enemy of the westering man. Every week, we got a new sheriff's sale of abandoned land. And always, cattlemen buy it up. It's easy for them to get land, even after it's been claimed. After six months desertion, any plot can be claimed by a new owner. The cattlemen buy up relinquishments—more men fail out here than make it. And for a fat bribe, the public officials let the land-grant settlers suffer at the hands of the cattlemen. They fence government land, fence off the public water holes, trample our crops.''

Bill nodded at the familiar story. Josh could see that Hickok was doing the same thing he had done with Elmer—he was *listening*. Listening, and observing both men for signs they were lying.

''In Kinkaid County,'' Hansen said bitterly, ''the word 'rustler,' has been stretched to include anybody who's not on a cattle payroll. A man of strong opinions, Mr. Hickok, is never forgiven. That's why my cousin Ned got killed. He's like me, he wouldn't shut up. Jesus Christ commanded us to smash the teeth of sinners, and like Ned, *I'm* a tooth-buster! I won't truck with criminals, and it's *criminals* that own Kinkaid County.''

Bill nodded, saying little. He thanked Hansen for his time, and promised the Swede he'd try to get to the bottom of this mess. As Josh and Bill rode back toward Progress City, Josh said, "Bill? Who you figure is lying? Kinkaid or Hansen?"

"Neither one," Bill replied cryptically. But no matter how hard Josh pressed him, Hickok would say no more.

Chapter Five

The wet, muddied, tired friends pounded their horses across the flats, fighting fitful rain squalls and harsh wind gusts. But they made it back to Progress City with time to spare before Bill's 8 P.M. poker game at the Medicine Bow. Josh had learned poker from watching Bill play, and was now a good hand himself. He meant to sit in tonight, as long as the stakes stayed low.

As usual, the horses were tended to first. Once nose bags full of crushed barley had been strapped to both mounts, Wild Bill and Josh soaked their rain-chilled limbs in hot baths, then filled their bellies at the town's only café.

The stormy weather and dark night had almost cleared the town's sole street. Still, Josh noticed that Bill kept forgetting to puff on his cheroot—a sure sign he expected trouble sooner rather than later.

"Kid," Wild Bill said as they crossed back to the hotel after supper, "remember to keep a weather eye out for Jane. I *know* she's around here. That woman is sneaky—and crazy as a shite-poke bird. And you can smirk all you want, Longfellow, but don't you forget. She's struck a spark for *you*, too."

Josh felt himself coloring like a bumpkin at the horrible memory of Bill's treachery down in Denver. With Calamity Jane about to barge in on Bill (who happened to be in a beautiful woman's boudoir at the time), Hickok had used Josh as a romantic distraction. He had in fact, as Josh accused him angrily afterward, "thrown an innocent Christian to a ravenous lion."

But Jane aside, neither did Wild Bill forget the more deadly threat to both men. When each of them headed to his own room just before the poker game, Bill said, "You got loads for that shooter I gave you?"

Startled, Josh nodded. Bill meant the old, but mint-condition, LeFaucheux revolver Bill had given him in Denver, shortly after Josh introduced himself to Hickok. The venerable French revolver required pin-fire cartridges, which could be difficult to find in smaller towns.

"Good," Bill said. "Stick six beans in the wheel, then strap the gun on in plain view. I've got what the mountain men used to call a God fear. It's been too quiet since we hit town. Tonight, somebody's going to put at us."

"Who?" Josh demanded.

Bill shrugged. "Where do all lost years go?" He left Josh standing alone in the hallway, gaping stupidly.

The saloon and gaming room attached to the hotel was small but comfortable, with green-baize card tables and fancy wallpaper patterned with gold fleur-de-lis. The nights still had a snap to them, and now red coals glowed inside the firebox of the stove.

Just before Jarvis Blackford came down from his room, the hotel clerk approached Wild Bill's table.

"What's the word, Yank?" Bill greeted the Civil War vet.

Jed Rault glanced around the nearly empty room. "Could be trouble shaping up, Wild Bill. Barry Tate, the foreman of the Rocking K, was in town earlier. He made a point of noising it all around that Wild Bill Hickok was in town—open reward and all."

Josh watched Bill mull this over while he riffled through a new deck of cards. "The ramrod of the Rocking K, huh? Hmm . . . tell me, Jed, you just an employee here?"

The clerk shook his head. "Part owner."

Bill frowned. "I was afraid of that. Look, there'll likely be some damage. But I will personally deliver the repair bill to Allan Pinkerton. That old skinflint is tighter than Dick's hatband, but he'll pay any bill I tell him to pay."

Jed nodded. "Your word's better than gold around me, Bill. Let 'er rip!"

* * *

"Wyoming," Jarvis Blackford said expansively, pouring Wild Bill another shot of bourbon. "It's a Delaware Indian term, you know. Means 'at the big plains.' "

"It's big, all right," Bill agreed as he studied his cards. "A man's got room out here to swing a cat in. But good land tends to draw a lot of boomers."

Bill spoke casually but chose those words deliberately. Josh studied Blackford's long, aristocratic face, but the man didn't blink an eye. "Boomers" was the frontier term of contempt for those who tried to be first on hand at every new settlement—those who simply cashed in and moved on, often a few steps ahead of the law.

As he always did, Wild Bill made sure his chair was placed against the wall. Josh knew that was not only to cover his back, but it left the entire room, and all in it, open to Bill's view.

"I've noticed," Jarvis commented while Josh dealt the next hand, "that you're a very cautious man, Wild Bill."

"I've learned a simple fact," Bill replied genially. "My existence is central to me, but it's only peripheral to others. I'll take three, kid."

Jarvis, busy scraping the bowl of his pipe with a pen knife, laughed outright. "Why, you're quite the philosopher, Bill!"

Josh could keep only half his mind on the game. Since Jed Rault's warning earlier, the youth had divided his attention between the saloon's few occupants and its two doors—one leading from the hotel lobby, another opening into the alley behind.

The game went forward, cards whispering, chips clinking, each man alive with his thoughts when Blackford wasn't expounding. Soon, it became apparent that Jarvis was again deliberately losing to Bill. Josh dropped out, remaining as dealer, when the ante rose to a dollar.

Still Bill went on winning. Hickok was purposely holding his cards so Josh could read them. Even when Bill intentionally killed three deuces, discarding to reduce them to a lowly pair, he *still* won.

Jarvis made a good pretense of being a real competitor. "Money in my pocket," he boasted each time he recklessly saw another raise. And he won now and then to make it look good. But Bill was right—the man was deliberately tossing his money down a rat hole. Why?

Again Josh's eyes swept the room, dwelling on both doorways. He could feel the awkward weight of the stiff leather holster on his right hip. Bill's words snapped in memory like burning twigs: *Tonight, somebody's going to put at us.*

Blackford, Josh abruptly realized, was talking to him.

"So *you* are the golden quill behind those stirring newspaper tales about Wild Bill? I can still recall your descriptions when you and Bill visited that Sioux village in Nebraska. Something about 'the beat of callused palms on a wet skin drum.' Quite vivid, lad. Makings of a Fenimore Cooper there."

Josh flushed with pride. Hell, maybe this Blackford

wasn't such a bad sort. The man clearly had good taste.

"The Philly Kid here," Bill tossed in, "is like a three-year-old colt. He's got his size and strength, but no sense yet to use them. See your dollar, Mr. Blackford, and raise you two more."

"Oh, the lad has sense, Bill. He was quite inspiring when he wrote, 'A man brave for one second can change the course of history.' Hear, hear! Bill Hickok has proved that point several times. But what do *most* men die for out here in the Wild West? To change history? Pah! For mince pie, that's what."

"It's what a man *lives* for that matters," Bill interjected amiably, speaking with a slim cheroot in his teeth. "I'll see you, and raise you two more."

"Speaking of what a man lives for, Bill . . ."

Blackford leaned forward on the table. His tone became a bit more intimate. "The West is finally starting to settle, thank the Lord. I can recall the day when women were so scarce out here a man had to marry whatever got off the train. Now we've got some real beauties. Gals like Nell Kinkaid. Seen her yet?"

"She's easy to look at," Bill agreed. "I'll take three, damnit," he added to Josh.

Josh had watched Blackford closely during this exchange about Nell Kinkaid. A slight movement of the older man's neck muscles suggested his remark was far from casual.

"Hit me, kid," Bill said, slapping down his discards.

"I'm fine," Jarvis told the young dealer.

Josh flipped two cards at Bill and set the deck down. Bill squinted to see through his cigar smoke, sorting out his hand. A moment later he slanted it so Josh could read it: a pair of aces and a pair of eights.

Aces and eights . . . Would Bill hold or fold? Josh wondered. Blackford hadn't taken even one discard. Since he wasn't one to bluff, that probably meant he had either a straight, a flush, or a full house. Any of which would beat a pair. On the other hand, Bill had been winning all night with far less in his hand.

The pot was up to ten dollars. Two days' wages for a Pinkerton op. He'll hold, Josh decided.

"Fold," Bill said promptly, tossing in his hand. And that's when Josh remembered what Bill had told him in Denver about aces and eights: *That hand has always been bad luck for me.* And in fact, as Josh realized later when it was all over, by folding just when he did, Wild Bill saved *both* their lives.

It turned out that Blackford also had only two pairs, sixes and nines. But precisely at the moment when Hickok *would* have been scooping in his winnings, it happened: Both doors leading into the saloon suddenly banged open hard.

Everything happened faster than a finger snap. But to Josh, who froze to the edge of his seat, it all had a dreamlike slowness to it, as if it were all happening underwater. He remembered the white-faced barkeep leaping under the counter. In the doorway behind the bar, Josh glimpsed a swarthy, heavyset man with hairy hands—hands clutching a Winchester repeater. Josh never even saw the other man.

Because he was not scooping in or stacking his winnings, Bill's hands were right where he always liked to keep them—thumbs on the seams of his trousers. Even before he had visual confirmation of his targets, Hickok had both guns out. Then he rolled off his chair, as the first rifle blasts splintered the wood.

Later that night Josh would write it exactly as it happened: "Wild Bill rolled three times, sat back on his heels, and emptied both Peacemakers in seconds, killing both would-be assassins." One stray rifle shot had snapped Blackford's fancy walking stick, and Bill's barrage of lead destroyed the back-bar mirror. But no one was hit besides the gunmen.

Jarvis Blackford, Josh saw immediately, was *not* part of this attack. His face had drained of color, and his hands trembled so that he couldn't even hold his pipe. Bill, in contrast, was calmly thumbing cartridges into his still-warm guns.

"Kid," he said sarcastically to Josh, "I taught you to shoot, but we'll have to work on your draw. I killed both those turkey buzzards before your gun cleared the holster. You're supposed to back me up, not bury me."

The barkeep ran to fetch Sheriff Waldo. Bill picked up his cheroot off the floor, stuck it in his teeth, and sat back down.

"Deal," he ordered Josh.

Chapter Six

Later that night, after the rain squalls had let up, a bitter-cold wind turned the soft mud to iron. While Wild Bill was keeping the undertaker busy in Progress City, homesteader Dave Hansen was hard at work in the chilly moonlight.

Despite the near-frozen ground and late hour, Hansen trudged up and down, up and down behind a plow with rusty shares. Because of the tense war lately in Kinkaid County, the big Swede was seriously behind in his work. Now he was plowing fire guards between his fields, anticipating moves by the cattlemen to burn him out as they had others.

For hours Hansen had been repeating the monotonous process—plowing long furrows and then burning the strips between them to keep flames from leaping. His cousin Ned, before finally being gunned down, had been burned out last summer during the dog days of August, when most of Wyoming would be natural tinder.

"Git! Git!" he shouted to his flagging dray horse. "One more row, Dobber, and then it's fresh oats. *Gee* up there, git!"

Normally Hansen would have been in bed hours before. But he had needed several plowing days lately just to repair his cut fences. Without them, Rocking K cowhands would deliberately haze cattle across his fields. Hansen wished to God he could find out *who* was poisoning cattle around here—it sure as hell wasn't him or any farmers he knew.

The wind still shrieked and howled like damned souls in torment. Hansen could hear little else above it as he shivered behind the plow. Thus, he had no warning at all before a loop of rope dropped over him and suddenly tightened, pinning his arms to his sides.

"Drag him over here, boys!" a voice shouted from the darkness. "Over here by this big cottonwood tree!"

Hooves thudded and Dave bounced along behind the horse like a helpless rag doll, pain grating through him.

"Goldang furriners!" somebody hollered. "Cow killers don't last long in Kinkaid County, Hansen!"

Fear numbed Hansen when one of the shadowy figures dropped a hangman's noose over his neck and tightened the coils against his windpipe. He watched his tormentor toss the other end of the rope over a thick tree limb. A scud of clouds blew away from the moon, and Hansen recognized one of the mounted tormentors despite the bandanna over his face.

"I know you, Barry Tate! I know those red sideburns!"

"Don't matter *what* you know, hoe-man. Don't matter a jackstraw!"

Three men had gathered around the other end of the rope. They tugged together, and Hansen was abruptly choked as he was pulled off the ground.

They didn't actually string him up—this time. Instead, Dave was pulled just off the ground and choked until he was on the verge of passing out. Then he was lowered for a few seconds before being hoisted aloft again.

While Dave watched, gasping, Barry Tate shifted his heavy weight, threw a leg around his saddle horn, and built himself a cigarette in the moonlight.

"You flea-bit farmers got a free ride west," Tate shouted. Hansen, like many local farmers, had come out west on the Northwestern Railroad, which gave free passes to the destitute. "And by God, you'll get a free ride back east—in a coffin!"

For about twenty minutes Hansen was jerked from the ground and held aloft, then lowered again briefly, choked to the verge of passing out. By the time his tormentors turned him loose, the farmer was coughing blood and struggling for breath.

"This is just dry-firing tonight," Tate assured the heap of twitching humanity that lay on the ground below him. "But you *will* stretch hemp, Swede, if you don't pull foot outta this territory. No farmers, sheepmen, nor coyotes welcome!"

Most people figured cows were stupid. But Johnny Kinkaid knew they could grow quite fond of their human handlers over time. He had heard beeves raise the dickens when separated from their drovers after a long drive.

So Johnny did feel sharp pangs of guilt as he twisted the cork stopper from a bottle of strychnine powder. He shook some into a metal washtub half filled with cool water. These cows in this far-flung holding pasture were especially thirsty. Johnny waited and watched, letting perhaps two dozen drink from the tub before he finally emptied it into the grass.

He knew from experience that all the animals that just drank would be dead within an hour. Though it troubled him deeply to poison his father's—and thus his own—cattle, the younger Kinkaid had finally squared with the facts.

The fact, for example, that Johnny was up to his goddamn ears in gambling debts, all owed to creditors in nearby Evansville and Barr Nunn. Or the fact that he was sick and tired of the hard, unpredictable life of a cattleman. Hell, a fortune made one year could all be lost during a hard freeze the next.

And now, like the answer to a prayer, Jarvis Blackford had arrived.

The railroad plutocrat was offering Johnny a life of *easy* wealth and comfort. Johnny knew his old man was decent, but Elmer Kinkaid was also a flintlock rifle in the age of the Winchester '72. Gone were the days when a man must work "from can to can't" to make his fortune. Nowadays, Johnny knew, a man got rich from speculation and investment—that is, by profiting off the hard labor of *others* without breaking a sweat himself.

For a moment, as he tied the washtub to one of his saddle straps, Johnny thought about Barry and the rest of the night riders. By now they should have thrown a good scare into that mouthy Dave Hansen.

Hansen. . . . Hickok rode out to his place earlier that day. But it wasn't the farmers around here who were paying Hickok. It was the cattle barons doing that. There was no proof, yet, that Hickok would mean trouble for Johnny.

But if he did, Johnny was *more* than ready to face Hickok in a gunfight—he was downright eager. Johnny could drop a silver dollar, then draw and fire his gun twice before that dollar hit the ground. As one awed admirer wrote in the *Progress City Beacon*, after watching Johnny win a county shooting match: "It's as if Johnny Kinkaid draws his gun today and fires it yesterday."

So let Hickok start turning over rocks, Johnny thought as he stepped up into leather. When it came time to post the pony, Johnny meant to be ready.

"This ain't factory ammunition, you young fool," Bill complained to Josh. "You bought reloaded shells! See where this one's been hand-crimped? They'll fire, but they won't be near as accurate."

Josh flushed and took the carton of .44 shells back from Wild Bill. "Sorry," he mumbled. "That's what the clerk gave me. I'll run get some of the right ones."

"Wasn't your fault, kid," Bill said, dismissing it. "Greenhorns are always an easy mark. We'll both walk over. You seen the local paper?"

Josh nodded. A front-page story—some of the most vivid details pulled from the very dispatch Josh had filed at the telegraph office—had added more information about Butch and Mike Labun, the brothers Wild Bill had killed the night before. A pair of dirty hard tails who used to make their living selling buffalo hides, until their ilk had almost wiped out the last herds.

"I'm thinking it likely had nothing to do with the war hereabouts," Bill said as the two men exited the Medicine Bow Hotel. Josh watched Wild Bill carefully survey the street along both sides. "Just a couple of lazy profiteers hoping to turn my bones into a fortune."

The two friends waited on the narrow boardwalk while several cowboys drove a small herd through town. A large bull started to peel away from the main gather. Abruptly, a puncher hazed it back by emitting the high-pitched Rebel yell from the war years.

Josh watched Bill start and actually begin to draw one of his Colts. Then Hickok shook his head.

"*Damn* but I'm glad I was a scout and spy during the war," he told Josh. "Being captured and tortured was rough. But *how* could the infantry face that damned, unnerving yell?''

The gun shop was on the other side of the street. The herd trailed out of town toward the east, and the two men crossed the still-muddy street. Bill exchanged the reloaded ammo for factory fresh, ignoring the stammering clerk's profuse apologies for ''the unfortunate mistake.''

They emerged just in time to see a fancy fringed surrey carefully negotiate the muddy ruts. The passenger was Nell Kinkaid, pretty in a yellow shirtwaist and a split buckskin riding skirt.

Josh and Bill touched their hats as the surrey drew near. Nell touched the driver's arm, and the surrey stopped in front of them.

''Well, Mr. Hickok!'' Nell called in her teasing manner. ''Already up to mischief, I see in this morning's paper. I suppose that means you'll be too busy to come visit me again?''

''Not at all, Miss Kinkaid,'' Bill replied gallantly. ''I've never found any real conflict between business and pleasure.''

At this, the driver scowled.

''Mr. Hickok,'' Nell added, ''this is Barry Tate, my father's foreman.''

Bill took the man in with one hard look. Not only was Tate wearing a .44 double-action Colt in a hand-tooled holster, but a Sharps .50 in a leather sheath lay on the seat beside him.

''I'm familiar with your work, Tate,'' Bill said in a toneless voice.

''How's that?''

''Last night I killed two of the boys you sicced on me.''

Nell, surprised, stared at the foreman.

''You're out of line, Hickok,'' Barry said.

''Next time,'' Bill added, ''send better men to do your killing for you.''

Josh watched Wild Bill again touch his hat to Nell before a red-faced Tate lashed the horse into motion.

''Man alive,'' Josh commented. ''That Tate looks mad enough to wake snakes.''

''There'll be plenty getting mad before I'm done with 'em,'' Bill promised as they headed back toward the hotel again. ''And some that are getting mad will be getting dead.''

Chapter Seven

Wild Bill paused in front of the door to his hotel room and placed his ear against it, listening carefully. He felt a curious sense of foreboding, but had to admit he had no solid evidence to justify it. Hearing nothing, he keyed the lock and swung open the door.

"Well, God kiss me!" he exclaimed.

Immediately, cold sweat broke out on Bill's temples. Calamity Jane sat on his bed, bold as Geronimo, patiently plaiting a bridle out of rawhide and horsehair. And Bill could tell from her lascivious leer that she was drunk as a fiddler's bitch.

"Bill Hickok, you hunk of virility! Honey bunch, I swear you're the purtiest man 'tween the Brazos and the Snake! Let Jane have a little sugar, you purdy lug!"

Jane began circling the room like a puma on the

prowl, Bill fleeing ahead of her. Jane's clumsy hobnailed boots left gray clumps of mud all over the rose-patterned carpet.

"How—how'd you know my room?" Bill asked her, stalling.

"Wal, I knew Wild Bill would never be stupid enough to stay in the room listed for him in the register. So I just sniffed for your cigar smoke—ain't many men who smoke them Cuba stinkers you like. Picked the lock with a horseshoe nail. Give us a little sugar, handsome!"

Bill barely managed to avoid her grasp. He ducked around one end of the bed. He knew he had to shake her before she got up a head of steam. Rumor had it Jane could wear out a mining camp full of men when she was in her cups.

"Now, Jane," he said in the soothing tone one uses with a dangerous horse, for Bill knew how quickly Calamity Jane could become offended. Once *that* happened, lead tended to fly. And with the exception of young Annie Oakley, no woman in America was a deadlier shot than Calamity Jane. "I have to leave right quick on business with the sheriff."

"You can run, Bill Hickok, but you can't hide—not from our shared destiny!" Jane held out her hand, pointing to a deep, dirty crease. "It's all right there, Bill. It's called the love line. See how deep and long mine is?"

Bill, backing away the entire time, almost tripped over a needlework stool. "Why, Jane. It—it looks like a rope scar to me."

''That line ain't the half of it,'' Jane insisted, pulling a sheet of dog-eared paper from her hip pocket and unfolding it. It was a diagram of a human head, covered with black dots.

''Ain't it the berries, Bill? I've had my skull read by a bumpologist,'' Jane declared, meaning a phrenologist. In 1872, phrenology—the ''science'' of interpreting personality from the shape of one's skull—was all the rage. ''He told me my love bump is special, the onliest of its kind. He told me only a very rare man can complete my romantic being. So there. It's been proved by them as knows! Me and you is *destined* to get hitched up, Bill. No sense fighting it.''

By now Bill felt trapped like a badger in a barrel.

''It's downright flattering, Jane,'' he told her. ''A comely lass like yourself. Why, if I wasn't a natural-born bachelor of the saddle, I'd be parking my boots under your bed.''

''You can run, Bill Hickok,'' she repeated. ''But you can't hide forever.''

By now Bill had circled the bed at least a dozen times. Desperate situations, he reminded himself, called for desperate remedies. One abruptly occurred to him.

''Jane, I've got to go see Sheriff Waldo right now. But you recall Joshua Robinson, don'tcha? He's the young fellow was with me in Denver. Josh is in the room at the end of the hall. In it *right now*.''

Jane's glassy eyes brightened at this intelligence. ''He's only a drumstick of a boy, ain't he? But dogs! He's cute as a bug's ear.''

"He was telling me," Bill said, "what a good-looking woman you are."

"He was?" Jane wasn't too drunk to be suspicious.

"Jane, would I lie to you? The lad told me, 'That Calamity Jane—a fellow could become a *man* with a woman like that to show him the ropes his first time.' "

"His first—Bill, do you mean that cute little parcel of manflesh ain't never had his clock wound?"

Bill nodded solemnly. "Each horse bucks to its own pattern, but he hasn't got a pattern yet. He's *willing*, God knows. But the right woman has yet to come along."

"That poor kid," Jane said, finally veering toward the door. "His ministering angel has come to earth."

"Hosanna on high!" Bill declared piously.

But before Jane, listing drunkenly, exited the room, she turned to Bill again. Now her homely face was dead serious.

"You keep an eye on your back trail, Bill Hickok, you hear me? There's a line shack north of here where a few jaspers have been meeting on the sly. And I'd bet a purty them ain't prayer meetings. More likely, they're figuring out a way to plant Bill Hickok."

Sheriff Carl Waldo was a likable, unequivocally fat man in his late thirties. Fine, sandy hair and a boyish face topped a massive body that would surely, Josh figured, sway a pony's back.

"Yessir, boys. Jesse Chisholm's dead now," the portly lawman reminisced. "But I was with him when he first pushed his cattle trail north to the first railheads. Gents, the West was wide open then. Big as a man's biggest dreams! Men ate beef off the hoof and didn't pay one red cent in taxes on it.''

Bill nodded. ''I pushed up Chisholm's trail myself as an Army scout, protecting herds bound for government reservations. Never had the pleasure of meeting Jesse. But I did visit his grave on that lonely hill in Geary, Oklahoma. I'll never forget the epitaph: 'No one left his home cold or hungry.' ''

''That was Jesse,'' Waldo agreed reverently. ''The 'man who fed America,' the newspapers called him. But ol' Jesse always took care to feed individuals, too. How you think *I* got this way?''

His visitors laughed. Then Bill got down to business, explaining that Pinkerton had sent him to Progress City to get to the bottom of the current ''county war.''

''There was more trouble last night,'' Sheriff Waldo informed the two men. ''On both sides. Dave Hansen came in this morning, said he was jumped last night while he was plowing fire guards. Had a big ol' rope burn on his neck, too. 'Bout the same time that happened, somebody poisoned another bunch of Elmer Kinkaid's cattle.''

The sheriff's office was hardly more than a closet with yellowing reward dodgers plastered to the walls. A drunk Indian was snoring in the tiny cell at the back. Through the room's single, fly-specked window, Josh could see ragged white parcels of cloud sliding across a sky the pure blue color of a gas flame.

But Josh was hardly in a mood to give a tinker's damn about the fine day. Less than an hour earlier, he had been forced to dive through the window of his hotel room, Calamity Jane cooing at his heels.

Bill asked Waldo, "Did Hansen say he recognized any of his attackers?"

The sheriff frowned. "Well, he *said* one of 'em was Barry Tate, ramrod of the Rocking K. But Dave's word alone don't amount to a hill of beans, Bill. You was a starman, you know that."

Josh watched Bill nod, mulling all this. Josh's impression was that Waldo was not a bad man so much as a dumb one. And though he was pro-cattle, like most western sheriffs, he didn't appear to be on their secret payroll. Bill called such men jackleg lawmen—they were decent enough, but completely untrained for their job.

Bill looked at Josh. "Could just be happen-chance, kid. But Dave Hansen was roughed up while we were playing poker with Blackford last night. That's when the cows were killed, too."

"That's been the way of it all along," Sheriff Waldo complained. "When one side hits, seems like the other does, too. A man tries to put handles on it, tries to parcel out the victims from the criminals. But it all runs together like juices on a Sunday plate. I admit I'm plumb bumfoozled."

As Bill had expected, Waldo was no help. But Hickok thanked him for his time and promised to keep in touch.

"Where to next?" Josh demanded when they were

outside again. "Christ knows the hotel ain't safe. Jane could still be waiting for us. *Us,* thanks to you, traitor."

"Now, kid," Bill said. "I wasn't looking for a sidekick, you begged to ride with me. And you agreed to bear my burden when you threw in with me. 'Member?"

"Sure, but I was talking about hardships. About danger. About ducking bullets and fists. Not about . . ." Josh shivered. "Not about *her.*"

Bill grinned, poked a cheroot into his teeth, and struck a match with his thumbnail to light it. Then he headed for the east edge of town, pulling Josh with him.

"Whatever doesn't kill you, Longfellow, can only make you stronger. C'mon."

"Where we going?"

"To the land office. And when I give you the word, I want you to keep watch out front, wouldja?"

"I guess. But why?"

" 'Cause I don't want anybody walking in on me, that's why. Now put a stopper on your gob and keep your eyes peeled for trouble."

"Yessir, Wild Bill," fawned Sam Watson, the land office clerk. "It's a real honor to have a visitor of your reputation. Touch you for luck, Bill?"

Josh knew Bill was hiding his irritation at this request. The story had grown, all through the American West, how Bill Hickok had escaped death far too often to be a mere mortal. Thus, many believed that simply touching him could bring good luck. Trouble was, it gave Bill a queasy feeling every time someone did—it forcefully reminded him he was long past due for the grave.

"My pleasure," Bill lied, reaching over the counter and giving the timid little clerk a hearty grip.

"Was there anything I could do for you, Bill?"

"Matter of fact, there is."

Bill nodded toward the long shelves behind Watson, loaded with dusty files. " 'Pears to me that you keep one of the most reliable sources of information in the county."

Josh watched Sam nervously toy with his green eyeshade. "Information, Bill?"

"Sure. You know who settled where, when. How much they originally paid for land versus the amount they sold it for. How much the land was improved, that type of thing."

"Well . . . that's so, Bill, that's so. Now, of course, them records're all official. They belong to the government, and by law no one can examine them."

"Why, of course," Bill agreed, pushing away from the counter. And when he did, Josh saw a shiny new five-dollar gold piece sitting there. "The only way a man *might* see those records would be behind your back. Say, if you stepped out to visit the jakes."

Josh watched the clerk stare at the shiner, licking his lips lightly.

"Actually," Watson said, "I ate some spoiled fruit yesterday, and now I've got the durned trots. Would you gents excuse me while I duck out back?"

Watson palmed the gold piece and headed outside.

"Get out front!" Bill snapped at Josh. "Sing out if anybody comes."

The door lock was flimsy. The moment Josh was outside, Bill tilted a chair under the doorknob. Then he vaulted the counter and made free with Watson's "government property."

The records of claim and transfer were neat and current. Only a brief examination was needed for Bill to grasp the larger pattern of settlement in Kinkaid County. In the first years, right after the Civil War, most filings went to homesteaders. But as time passed, the pattern shifted: far more sections were transferred to cattlemen.

But more interesting: Elmer Kinkaid's name appeared on none of the later claims. Instead, Barry Tate and Johnny Kinkaid were concentrating on acquiring one section along Turk's Creek—a section thick with homesteaders. Obviously the water rights were the issue. But oddly—Turk's Creek was *not* a convenient water source for the Rocking K. Given its location, even irrigation ditches would not make it a practical source. So why this concentrated effort to acquire that tract of land?

"Wild Bill?" came Watson's timid voice from out back. "Am I through out here?"

"C'mon in, Sam," Bill called, vaulting the counter again. "You didn't see a thing, chappie."

"No, sir, I never do!"

Bill set the chair back, let himself out, then headed back toward the hotel with Josh in tow.

"What'd you find out, Bill?" Josh demanded.

"That the world is not honest," Bill said, deliberately frustrating Josh. "Now we got to find out if Jane has cleared out yet."

She had, Jed Rault informed the two relieved guests. Both men headed back toward Bill's room.

"Here's the way of it, kid," Bill said as he fished out his key and turned it in the lock. "According to the land records, government ground that once sold for a buck twenty-five an acre is now selling for thirty dollars an acre. Yet it's sitting unused. Why?"

Josh watched Bill ease open the door, quickly check the room, then step inside. Josh moved in right behind him.

"Jane must've come in the window," Bill remarked, and Josh saw the lace curtains blowing inward. Bill normally kept that window shut and covered. He was crossing the room to close it now when, quick as a finger snap, something flew through the window and thunked hard on the floor, rolling under the bed.

Josh glimpsed sparks spraying, heard a hissing, spitting noise, and his stomach turned to ice when he realized the object was a stick of lit dynamite!

Chapter Eight

''Man alive!'' Josh exclaimed, even as he turned to dive back out into the hallway.

But in his panic Josh miscalculated. His left shoulder whumped hard into the doorjamb. Josh promptly ricocheted back into the room. And when he did, he bowled over Wild Bill, who was trying to escape right behind him.

Both men landed in the middle of the floor in a confused heap of limbs. The dynamite, meantime, still spitting and fizzing, rolled on out from under the bed and stopped only inches from Bill's outstretched hand.

''Oh, hell,'' Josh heard him say calmly, as if he'd messed up knotting his tie. A moment later, Bill gripped the stick and hurled it back out the window.

The resulting explosion in the street rocked the hotel and sent dirt slapping into the room.

"I just saved Pinkerton one hell of a bill," Hickok boasted as he cautiously edged up to the window and looked outside.

"See anybody?" Josh demanded when he could speak again.

"Plenty of surprised faces," Bill told him. "But none of them looks guilty."

An ashen-faced Jed Rault appeared in the doorway. "You gents still in one piece?"

"Still sassy, Jed," Bill told the desk clerk. "And you got a new water hole out front. Any chance we can move me into a new room later?"

"You bet, Wild Bill. Good God Almighty!"

"That tears it," Bill announced after Rault had returned to the hotel lobby. "The war kettle is on the fire, kid. It wasn't reward seekers who tossed that dynamite. Bounty hunters would likely choose a cleaner way to kill me so they could prove the identity of the body."

"So it's likely one side or the other in the county war," Josh concluded. "But which one?"

Bill skinned the wrapper off a cheroot, rolling that question around in his mind. "That's one nut we ain't cracked yet. There's more evidence pointing to the cattle faction. But evidence ain't proof. And even if it is the cattlemen, it don't seem likely they'd *all* be in the mix. We need to sort the grain out from the chaff. C'mon, kid."

"Where we going, Wild Bill?"

"Another visit with Elmer Kinkaid. But first we stop at the Western Union office. I think it's high time we start asking some questions about Mr. Jarvis Blackford—*if* that's his real name. I got a hunch it's what we call a 'summer name' in the West."

"So who is he?"

"Jesus, kid, am I a soothsayer? But I know damn good and well he's not deliberately losing at cards because he despises money. And how come the busiest times for night riders come when I'm playing cards with him?"

Bill locked his door again.

"Yeah, but Bill," Josh protested, "if Blackford—"

Bill, lost in speculation, raised one impatient hand. "Kid, say little and miss nothing," he snapped. "You yap way too goddamn much. It gives me a headache."

Before the two friends recruited their horses at the livery stable and rode out to the Rocking K spread, they stopped by the telegraph office. Bill knew that Allan Pinkerton was a living catalogue of the rich and famous in America—especially the movers and shakers in the rapidly expanding railroad business. Bill wired Pinkerton a meticulous description of the man called Jarvis Blackford.

The day was sunny, bright, and windy, the cold wave of the night before long gone. The meadows were bright with blue columbine and white Queen

Anne's lace. Purple sage carpeted the open flats where grass grew scant.

"Bill?" Josh said when they had ridden perhaps halfway. "Those two hard tails you killed at the hotel—did you see in the paper this morning there's going to be an auction to sell their horses?"

" 'Course I did, kid. That's the custom in the West when a town is forced to bury a man. You sell his horse to cover expenses. That's one reason I quit being a lawman. I got sick of holding all those damned sheriff's sales."

The two horsebackers topped a long ridge and could see the beautiful Haystack Valley opening out below them. Josh saw Bill stare intently, and he followed his gaze: the frontiersman was watching the diamond stack of a locomotive in the distance, barreling along at a breakneck speed of thirty-five miles per hour on the Northwest Line, sparks flying from the hot stack.

"The sun travels west," Bill muttered thoughtfully. "And so does the railroad."

But before Josh could press Bill on this cryptic utterance, the older man squeezed his roan with his knees and the big gelding leaped forward. They covered the rest of the distance to the Rocking K at a lope.

The scene at the Kinkaid spread was much as they'd found it last time. A wrangler was breaking a horse to leather in a pen near the house, its head covered with burlap to slow its bucking. Behind the house, several disgruntled cowboys had been forced to trade lariats for posthole diggers, making holes for a new fence.

"How's by you, Wild Bill?" Elmer greeted his famous visitor after the maid showed the men in. "I reckon you know by now I had a bunch more beeves poisoned?"

Bill nodded to the wheelchair-bound old man. "And maybe you know that some local waddies roughed up Dave Hansen?"

"Well, that just goddamn makes me cry," Elmer said sarcastically. "Why would cattlemen do that to a cow killer, I wonder?"

Josh had discreetly been looking for the beautiful Nell Kinkaid. So far, however, he saw no sign of her.

"Hansen denies killing any beeves," Bill pointed out.

"Simon Peter denied Christ, too, Bill! You believe *him*?"

Wild Bill laughed at that one. The old patriarch had a mind like a steel trap despite his bent and broken body.

"Elmer," Bill said bluntly, "tell me, why are Barry Tate and your boy Johnny filing on so many homestead claims? Buying them outright, buying up relinquishments, even using soldier's widows to acquire clear titles?"

Elmer, taken by surprise by all this, twisted a finger into his soup-strainer mustache. "The hell you talking about, Hickok?"

Bill candidly confessed that he had illegally examined the records at the land office in Progress City.

He told Elmer how Barry and Johnny were clearly trying to acquire complete ownership of a key stretch of Turk's Creek—currently settled by homesteading farmers.

"You sure on all this?" Elmer demanded.

"Sure as we're sitting here, Elmer."

"I don't understand it," Elmer said wonderingly. "God strike me down if I do! What Barry does is *his* beeswax. I 'magine the man is somehow putting by against the future. But Johnny? Hell, he's already in line to inherit thousands of acres when I pass away. And Turk's Creek? Why, hell. It's good water, but useless to the Rocking K. It's way out past the hard-table fringe."

Elmer fell silent abruptly, as if he'd been slugged. Josh watched him wipe sweat off his forehead with the back of his wrist. Clearly this revelation had struck the old-timer like a bolt out of the blue.

"I'm not trying to build a pimple into a peak," Bill assured the rancher. "And I know who's paying my salary. But so far, Elmer, it looks to me like *your* side is more sinning than sinned against. Even despite all your dead cattle."

Josh could tell that this news about Johnny was starting to really sink in deep. The first flush of surprise had passed, and anger rushed in to take its place. For a moment, Elmer was so furious his facial bones seemed to stand out and his eyes to sink in.

Josh rose from his chair in alarm when the old man's breathing suddenly became ragged. Bill was even quicker.

"Where's the liquor cabinet, Elmer?" he demanded, even as he opened the top button of the old man's shirt.

"Room at end . . . end of hallway," Elmer managed.

"Watch him," Bill ordered Josh.

Hickok hit the long hallway at a run. But there were two doors at the end, one on either side. Bill flung open the door on the right, then sucked in a hissing breath of surprise.

Warm steam billowed into his face, and a pleasant odor like lilacs and honeysuckle. Nell Kinkaid, naked as Eve in Paradise, was just then rising from a claw-footed washtub. Bill glimpsed high, firm breasts with huge strawberry-colored nipples, a pert little bottom taut and smooth as polished wood.

At the very first sound of the door, Nell flinched like a startled doe. Then she just stood there boldly matching Wild Bill's stare, her dark eyes flashing.

"Is this an accident, sir?" she finally demanded, still making no effort to cover her nakedness. She stood as still as a hound on point.

"It is, Nell," Bill replied, his temples throbbing with stirred-up blood. "But I refuse to apologize, because I *don't* regret it."

"I don't want you to," she assured him. "Or I'd have covered up by now." Nell finally did hold a towel in front of her. "Au revoir," she told him playfully, blowing Bill a kiss. "*Think* about this, Mr. Hickok."

"Oh, it'll lead my thoughts," Bill assured her, regretfully backing out of the room. The other door led to Elmer's den. By the time Bill returned with a bottle of rye and a jolt glass, Elmer looked half alive again.

"Didn't mean to go puny on you, boys," Elmer assured his visitors after he'd tossed back a shot. "That son of mine would drive a saint to poteen. But I love him. He's the only boy I got, you know. I love him, but I know there's a hole in him somewhere."

Josh knew Bill had more questions for the elder Kinkaid, but the rancher was in no shape for more rough handling right then. Bill asked for directions to the north-boundary line shack, then the visitors left.

They were trotting out of the main yard when a six-gun suddenly barked several rapid shots. This was followed by an explosion of whistles and cheers.

Josh and Wild Bill slued around in their saddles to glance back. An arrogant-looking, handsome young man with wavy brown hair sat on the top rail of a corral, thumbing reloads into a six-gun. A cowboy rode past him at breakneck speed on a fast little coyote dun. The puncher was twirling a knotted rope as quickly as he could while riding full-bore.

Josh knew that could only be Johnny Kinkaid sitting on the corral rail. Kinkaid fired six rapid shots, and each time he did, one more knot flew off the rope. More cheers rose from the hands witnessing this. Josh could tell that Bill, too, was impressed.

"Colonel Cody would pay good money to get him in his Wild West show," Bill observed thoughtfully.

They rode a few more paces. Then Bill met Josh's

eye again. He tilted his head back toward the corral.

"Respect that gun, kid, if not Kinkaid himself. We don't take care, he'll have *both* of us walking with our ancestors."

Chapter Nine

"You're *still* harping about avoiding a confrontation?" Johnny Kinkaid demanded. "Even after what Hickok did to the Labun brothers?"

Johnny, Barry Tate, and Jarvis Blackford had again met in the deserted line shack to coordinate their strategy like battlefield generals. Blackford knocked the dottle out of his pipe, speaking with his usual, imperturbable calm.

"Johnny, I consider your old man one of the smartest stags on the range. And you've inherited the full ration of his brains. But you've got to rein in that hot streak in you, son. The cat *sits* by the gopher hole, he doesn't rush in."

" 'Sides," Barry chipped in, "what Hickok done to the Labuns ain't our mix, Johnny. They was looking to cash in, and he shot them in self-defense."

"My point exactly," Blackford agreed. "Johnny, you say Wild Bill's been out to your place twice now. That's good. If he was turning on the cattlemen, he'd more likely keep his distance."

"Unless," Johnny pointed out, "he's only coming around on account he's bird-dogging my sister Nell."

At this suggestion, Barry scowled while Jarvis smiled with pleasant surprise.

"All the better," Jarvis insisted. "Puts him in the family, so to speak. *Is* he after her?"

" 'Pears so. Nell ain't one to go giddy over a pair of pants. But she's caught a spark for Hickok. Came back from town yesterday with a stack of dime novels about him. At dinner every night, her mouth runs six ways to Sunday about how 'fascinating' the man is."

Johnny's goading eyes cut to Barry. "Top of all that, she give ol' Barry here the go-by last night when he invited her to the county fair in Evansville next week. After going with him the past three years. Ain't that the straight, Barry?"

The foreman clamped his teeth around his first retort. He clenched his jaw so tight, the muscles bunched. Barry had already publicly filed his claim to Nell Kinkaid. That made any man who moved in on him a claim jumper. Trouble was, Hickok wasn't just *any* man.

"Well, the main point," Jarvis reminded the other two, "is that nobody in power can find flies on us, Hickok included. The man is definitely suspicious of me, but that's his job. He made a few cagey remarks during our last card game, but he was fishing, is all."

"I don't give a hang *what* he's doing," Johnny protested, his face twisted with insolence. "It just ain't smart to leave a man as dangerous as Hickok free to nose around at will. That bastard could turn on us quicker than an Indian steals a horse. Don't forget that newspaper brat—he could noise our plan all over the damned country."

"He'd have to know what we're really up to," Blackford pointed out. "And *nobody* can know that, not yet. The Burlington is just now moving the first surveying and grading crews in. There aren't a dozen men who know about this new spur line yet, and they're all closemouthed railroad barons."

"It's a mistake to trust Hickok," Johnny insisted stubbornly. "That bastard will see we get the hind teat. You know how much money I got tied up in this plan?"

"Who said anything about *trusting* him?" Jarvis retorted. "For that matter, did I ever say we should let Hickok live? I only said we must be careful how we kill him."

This teasing hint tantalized both of his companions. They watched Blackford serenely puff on his fancy pipe, enjoying his moment of suspense.

"Well?" Johnny demanded. "We got to play three guesses? How you mean to kill Hickok?"

"As you both know, I'm in the hotel with him and that young ink-slinger. Hickok likes to play coy and switch rooms. But there's a Chinese kid that runs the bathhouse behind the hotel. He also cleans the rooms every day and knows where Hickok *really* is. I've got the kid on our payroll. That's how I knew which room your men should dynamite."

"Fat lot of good it did."

"Patience, Johnny, patience. Hickok's clover is deep, but the man is mortal. We'll come up with a plan, and we *will* sink that arrogant son of a bitch. Just stay the course for now. All three of us are going to get rich. So rich we'll need lawyers just to tote up how much we have. And the famous Wild Bill Hickok will soon be feeding worms."

Josh watched Wild Bill carefully spread out his duster before he flopped on his belly to drink from a little runoff stream. Bill spat out the first mouthful, then drank deeply. Josh imitated him.

It was late in the forenoon on the day after their latest visit to Elmer Kinkaid. The two men were riding up into the high-ground summer pastures where the north-line shack was located. Wild Bill knew Calamity Jane was a drunkard, and even a mite touched. But she had uncanny frontier survival instincts. If she mentioned that shack to him, then it was worth the trouble of checking it out.

The sun was bright, the air cool, and the country hereabouts bursting with the wild beauty following the annual snowmelt. The riders ascended through meadows where sunflowers grew shoulder high, and blue-wing teals darted about like spring-drunk butterflies.

Josh had tried firing questions at Bill ever since they rode out of Progress City after breakfast, but

Wild Bill was full of his own thoughts, either ignoring the kid altogether or snapping at him to "put a sock in it, wouldja?" At no time did Hickok relax his habitual vigilance. The fathomless eyes were everywhere, missed nothing.

Halfway up a long slope, the riders encountered another bunch of poisoned cattle. Josh counted twenty bulls, cows, and dehorned yearlings.

"This time it's the Circle B brand," Bill announced after shooing flies away with his hat to read the brand. "According to the map Pinkerton gave us, that's the spread just west of Elmer's."

Josh watched Bill step into the stirrup, then swing up and over. He kicked his roan forward.

"Speaking of Pinkerton," Josh said, pressuring with his knees to start the *grullo* behind Bill. "Any reply yet to your telegram about Jarvis Blackford?"

"Haven't had time to check yet," Bill replied. "I meant to go this morning, but I had to change hotel rooms when one opened up. We'll stop at the telegraph office after we stash our horses. Hallo, Longfellow! There's our line shack. Cover down. Ride behind the trees from here."

Both men entered a stand of box-elder trees and moved to within thirty feet of the weather-beaten shack.

"Looks deserted," Bill said. "But let's tie up here and sneak in. And don't forget—I *think* Jane has cleared out of this area, but I'm not sure of that."

This reminder made Josh's scalp crawl. Like Bill,

he had learned there was a limit to the dangers a man could actually shoot.

They ground-hitched their mounts and moved in closer, leapfrogging from tree to tree. A thin, nearly transparent hide had been stretched tight over the shack's only window. But it was torn in one corner. Bill sneaked close, looked inside, then called out to Josh, "No one's home, kid. C'mon."

The packed dirt in front of the shack was plastered with horseshoe prints. So many that Josh couldn't make sense of them.

Bill, however, squatted and quietly studied the ground for several minutes.

"Three riders have been meeting here," Wild Bill finally announced. "They've met several times, a few days between each meeting. Two are cattlemen and ride cow ponies. See that flat forge-mark? Cow ponies wear a rounder, flatter shoe for quick turns and twists. The third man is riding a big, heavy horse, at least seventeen hands, wearing high-crowned shoes. The kind they forge in big cities and put on boarded horses."

Josh was thoroughly impressed by all this. Wild Bill had "read" the ground the way Josh used to read Homer! Hickok might hate to get his clothes dirty, but there wasn't a better scout or tracker in the West, Josh reminded himself.

"Which means," the *New York Herald* reporter translated, "two locals meeting with an outsider."

Bill nodded and moved inside the shack. It didn't take long to look around the cramped hovel.

''All those dead matches,'' Bill said, pointing to a scattering on the floor. ''But no butts. And the matches all burned more than halfway.''

''Pipe smoker,'' Josh supplied. ''Jarvis Blackford!''

Again Bill nodded. ''Doesn't tell us much, does it? But then again, it's nice to know. I think we best visit the Western Union office, Longfellow. Mr. Jarvis Blackford may be a much better gambler than we realize.''

But before the two riders made it back to Progress City, trouble crossed their trail yet again.

Wild Bill and Josh were still about two miles north of town, approaching from behind a long ridge to minimize target opportunities for any snipers. They crested the ridge, then Bill suddenly reined in.

''Hold it, kid. Look down in the valley.''

Josh did. It didn't take long to assemble the picture. A farmer wearing a floppy-brimmed hat was tied to a tree. His mule lay dead in the traces, still hitched to the plow. Several cowhands were busy tearing down the barbed-wire fence around a huge section of plowed ground.

Now and then, as the two men cautiously rode closer, Josh heard a cracking snap—a cowhand was laying into the prisoner with a whip that had a wicked leather lash.

''This dog and pony show is over,'' Bill said quietly. A second later, a pearl-grip Peacemaker was in his right fist. Bill fired once, and the lash flew off the whip.

All heads snapped around to see who the new arrivals were. One of the cowhands started to raise his Winchester. Bill's Colt barked again, and Josh heard the cowboy let out a bleat of alarm as the rifle fell to the ground.

"He shot off my damn trigger finger!" the cowboy exclaimed.

Josh, too, had drawn his pinfire revolver. But no one paid any attention to him. They knew damn well who the blond-haired, steel-eyed *hombre* with the fancy shooters must be. Now that they had ridden closer, Josh recognized the bushy red burnsides on the man holding the ruined whip: Barry Tate. So those cowboys ruining the fence must be Rocking K hands.

Tate dropped the whip and stood with his hands balled on his hips. "The hell you doing poking in here, Hickok?" he demanded as if he had a right to know.

Josh saw Bill's gaze shift to the beleaguered farmer. He slumped forward against his ropes, shoulders hunched as if to ward off wind. He was an older man, perhaps nearing fifty, his face raw from soap and wind.

"Cut him loose," Bill told Tate with quiet authority.

Tate watched the two mounted men from his shifty, horse trader's eyes. "He's a rustler, Hickok!"

"Sure he is," Bill replied. "And I'm the Apostle Paul. Nothing ruins truth like stretching it, Tate. You cattlemen yell 'rustler,' then sweep the ranges clear of all hoe-men. I said cut him loose."

At this, Tate made an impatient noise in his throat. "Nerve up, damnit, alla yous!" he hollered at his men. "There's only two of them!"

Barry's arithmetic was accurate. But one of those two was Wild Bill Hickok. Nobody, including Tate, went for a weapon. One of the waddies hustled to untie the farmer.

"What's your name, friend?" Bill asked the grateful old man.

"Peatross. Lonnie Peatross."

"If anything else happens to Mr. Peatross here," Bill shouted so all could hear, "Wild Bill Hickok will *personally* settle the score. Mr. Peatross, what'd you pay for that mule?"

"Forty dollars, Wild Bill."

"Pass the hat, boys!" Hickok shouted to the Rocking K hands. "Either you give this man forty dollars, or I shoot every one of your horses!"

"Now just a goddamn minute here, Hickok," Tate blustered. "We don't hafta—"

"Shut your fish trap, Tate, and keep it shut. I'll make the medicine around here, and you'll *take* it."

Bill glanced up at the westering sun. "Work quick, boys! You can have that fence back up by sundown."

A shocked silence followed this incredible order. The hands all stared at Barry. Barry, in turn, stared at the sun reflecting off Bill's pearl grips.

"Get to work!" Tate finally shouted. But Josh had never seen such hatred in a man's eyes.

"You're in deep soup, Hickok," he said before he turned away.

"Think so?" Josh watched Bill slide a cheroot from his vest and shuck off the wrapper. "Know what, Tate? I think I'll steal your woman from you and humiliate you in front of all your men. Then I think I'll kill you to end your misery."

Bill had said all this in a low, pleasant voice. Tate whirled back around, so enraged his eyes protruded like wet marbles. Bill wagged one of his Colts.

"You're burning daylight, Barry. Get to work. I don't leave until you boys have finished the job."

But Tate got the last word.

"As to finishing the job," he assured Bill, "you ain't even met Johnny Kinkaid yet. He'll kill you deader than a Paiute grave! *That*'ll finish the job, all right."

Chapter Ten

Thanks to his unscheduled stop at Lonnie Peatross's farm, Wild Bill didn't make it back to Progress City before the Western Union office had closed for the day. But next morning, immediately after a piping-hot breakfast of potatoes, eggs, and side meat, Bill and Josh visited the telegraph office.

"Yes *sir*, Mr. Hickok," said a fawning telegrapher, turning to a pigeonholed wall behind him. "A message came in for you late yesterday off the Denver trunk line. I sent a boy over to the hotel, but Jed Rault said you were out."

Behind the clerk, a sounder began tapping out an incoming message in Morse code. The clerk ignored it, for a new invention—the perforation drum—picked it up in printed code for later transcription.

The clerk handed Wild Bill a folded yellow message form. Josh watched Bill quickly unfold it, read it, then fold it again and look at the clerk. Bill seemed to be studying his face, as if trying to read his character, the way he read those prints in front of the shack.

"What's your name?" Bill asked him.

"Roundtree, Wild Bill. Jimmy Roundtree."

"Jimmy, did you take down this message?"

The clerk nodded.

"Are you a Christian, Jimmy?"

The clerk goggled at Hickok. "Why . . . yessir. Yessir, I believe I am."

"Good. Then I'm asking you—swear to God now—if you've mentioned this to anyone?"

The clerk raised his right hand and said solemnly, "Bill, may God strike me *and* my family dead if I've said a word to anybody. And I won't, either."

"Good man."

"Touch you for luck, Bill?" the clerk said hopefully as the two visitors were about to leave. Bill not only gave the clerk a hearty grip, he poked a cartridge out of his shell belt and plunked it down on the counter. Bullets even rumored to be from Hickok's very own belt had sold as high as $20.

"*Ho*-ly moly! *Thanks*, Bill! I mean it, thanks!"

Josh had trouble containing his curiosity. Bill had folded the message and tucked it into his vest without a word. Out on the boardwalk again, Josh watched a peddler's wagon rattle through town. It reminded him of Calamity Jane's outlandish conveyance. In front of the blacksmith shop, a sweating forgeman was warping a tire around a wheel.

"Well?" Josh finally demanded.

Without a word, Bill handed his friend the message form. While Josh read Pinkerton's telegram, Bill kept a wary eye on the surrounding doorways and windows.

PHYSICAL DESCRIPTION YOU SENT JOGGED NO MEMORY UNTIL YOU MENTIONED WALKING STICK AND PIPE. THEY ARE DEAD GIVEAWAYS. HAS TO BE RICHARD STRICKLAND. FORMER TOWNSITE PLANNER WHO NOW WORKS FOR THE BURLINGTON RAILROAD AS A "PROJECT DEVELOPMENT CONSULTANT." MAN IS VALUED FOR HIS ABILITY TO CLEAR THE PROFIT PATH OF ALL THAT BLOCKS IT. SORRY I DON'T KNOW WHAT HE'S UP TO. BUT HE'S INFINITELY RESOURCEFUL, SO USE EXTREME CAUTION.

Josh handed the message back to Wild Bill.

"I had a hunch old 'Jarvis' is a railroad plutocrat," Hickok said. "It doesn't tell us what exactly he's up to, but he sure as hell ain't selling bolts and screws out at that line shack—just one hell of a swindle of some kind. Next time we ride, Longfellow, we'll go poke around Turk's Creek, see what we can see."

* * *

Calamity Jane bit off a corner of plug and soon had it juicing proper. She watched a cow puncher ride hard past her secret camp, a willow copse that covered the lee of a small ridge. It was the middle of the afternoon, and Jane was nursing the mother of all hangovers. Several empty bottles of Doyle's Hop Bitters surrounded Jane's bedroll.

"Well, cuss my coup," she croaked at her team, tethered nearby and taking off the grass. "That rider is one of them that's been palavering at the line shack. They just had 'em a meetin' yestiddy. Them buzzards're up to no good, or I'll eat my John B. Stetson!"

Despite the mule kicking inside her skull, Jane forced herself to her feet. Her clothes were itchy with beggar lice. She pulled the big Volcanic pistol from her sash and swung open the loading gate to check the wheel.

"Let's go, General Custer," she said to a horse with a gorgeous long blond mane. "That rider had a look on his face that was death to the devil! I got the fantods about Bill. We best dust our hocks back to the shack."

Jane's team were combination horses, broke to saddle or tug chains. Jane kept a saddle, pad, and bridle in her buckboard. She rigged General Custer, wincing at the exploding pain in her head every time she tightened a latigo or stretched a cinch.

"Lord, the trials I suffer for that man," Jane said out loud. "Bill Hickok is my cross to bear, I reckon. He's bound and determined to get hisself kilt. And

I'm bound and determined to get that purty man nekked in my bedroll first.''

''You see?'' Johnny Kinkaid demanded. ''You *see* it? I warned you that bastard Hickok would turn on us like a rabid dog! He's been writ up in books and newspapers so often it's made him prideful as a damned rahjah. He don't even respect the cattlemen paying his wages. You heard what Barry said—yesterday Hickok even shot Danny Ford's trigger finger off!''

''That ain't the half of it,'' Barry Tate said, his face closed and bitter in the dim light of the shack. Barry had been hazing cattle earlier, and now he still wore his roping gloves. ''Hickok made us cough up forty bucks for Peatross's spavined mule! And then he put us to work for over an hour—under the gun.''

The man who called himself Jarvis Blackford raised both hands like a priest blessing his flock. ''Would you two please stop all the calamity howling? I assure you, our coals haven't turned to ashes yet, boys. Far from it.''

Johnny impatiently shifted his shell belt. ''Assure a cat's tail! I warned you about letting Hickok live. Every damn thing we've worked for could get shot out of the saddle just like''—Johnny snapped his fingers—''*that*. We can't wait, I'm telling you. The sooner we kill Hickok, the better!''

''And I'm working on doing just that,'' the older man assured him. ''But this 'urgent meeting' you boys demanded is jeopardizing the effort.''

"How so?" Johnny demanded.

"There's only so many hours in a day, son! Tonight I'm playing poker again with Hickok. But I'm also supposed to meet the Chinese kid and get Wild Bill's new room number. The time to strike is now, right after he's moved in and when he's feeling safest. You boys can ride into town later and wait in my room. I'll send the kid to you with the room number. You could be waiting for Hickok when he comes back from playing cards."

After the three men had ridden out, Calamity Jane quickly rose from the ground, kneecaps popping. She had been stretched out prone behind the shack, her ear to a big crack between two boards.

"Wall, I'll be hung for a horse thief!" she told General Custer as she grabbed leather and heaved herself into the saddle. "Them dirty sons of whores! Bill Hickok will dance over their bones!"

Three sharp raps sounded on Josh's door.

"Shake a leg, junior," Bill's voice called from the hallway. "Time for me to collect my free money."

Josh threw the door open for Bill, then finished slicking back his hair in front of a warped mirror.

"You should use axle grease, kid," Bill admonished him, wrinkling his nose. "That bay rum tonic smells like a French whore. C'mon—let's see how many ways 'Mr. Blackford' can deliberately ruin a winning hand tonight."

"Should I bring my gun?" Josh asked. It hung from a peg on the back of the door.

"Sure. But if we have to bust caps," Bill teased, "try to get it out of your holster sometime before my funeral."

Josh scowled as he buckled on the vintage French pistol. His Quaker mother back in Philadelphia would have a hissy fit if she knew her boy was toting a weapon. And now Bill was still roweling him about that surprise attack from the Labun brothers.

"But that all happened so quick," Josh objected. "Why, man alive! It was over in an eyeblink."

"It always is, kid. That's why you've gotta be *faster* than an eyeblink. When trouble comes, a man has to react *with* it, not after it, y'unnerstan'?"

By now both men were in the narrow hallway, following a threadbare carpet toward the saloon in one wing of the hotel.

"Curious, ain't it?" Wild Bill asked Josh. "Ol' Jarvis not only lost a mint playing poker with me—he damn near got a few air shafts in him when the Labun boys tried to snuff my candle. Yet he *still* wants to play. Sorta makes you wonder, don't it, what's his big idea for tonight?"

Before Josh could answer, a skinny Chinese kid with an ugly carbuncle on his neck emerged from a room ahead of them, pushing a mop bucket. Josh recognized him as the same kid who kept the hot-water boiler stoked in the bathhouse out back.

Bill nodded at the kid and he nodded back, hustling to get the bucket out of Hickok's path. Shortly after the two friends went into the saloon, still talking, the man calling himself Jarvis Blackford descended the stairs at the end of the hall. He stopped near the Chinese worker and glanced around to make sure they were alone.

''Where is he?'' Blackford asked quietly.

''Seven,'' the kid replied.

Blackford nodded and handed the kid a silver dollar. ''Take that information to the two men waiting up in my room.''

Then Blackford headed toward the saloon to meet Wild Bill Hickok.

''Dirty, white-livered, back-shooting sons of bitches,'' Calamity Jane muttered to herself as she pushed General Custer toward Progress City. ''See how them scum-suckers like it when I spoil the surprise for 'em! Bill will shoot them bastards into rag tatters! Hold on, pretty Bill! Jane's a-comin'!''

Jane was a fair-to-middling horsebacker when she was sober. But now, with hangover fumes still clouding her vision and slowing her reflexes, she was pushing General Custer too fast in unknown country. Thus she wasn't aware, at first, when they crossed into a little hollow pockmarked with gopher holes.

By the time Jane realized her danger, it was too late. General Custer shifted hard right, then fell down fast when he plunged his right foreleg into a gopher hole. Jane flew head-over-handcart, her head striking a tree limb hard.

She saw a bright-orange explosion inside her skull. By the time she flopped to the ground, rolling fast, she was out cold.

Chapter Eleven

"Wealth," Jarvis Blackford lectured in his polished baritone voice, "should depend on achievement, not birth. *That's* the American way."

"That's quite true," Wild Bill agreed as he flipped eight bits into the pot, anteing up. "But 'achievement' is a pretty broad word, huh? Takes in everything from murder to extortion."

"A good point," Blackford said patronizingly. "And I'm caught upon it, sir! Of course, I meant *honorable and legal* achievements."

"Of course," Bill said politely.

"Now, for example. Wild Bill, I'm told the man who kills you will receive ten thousand dollars from an angry father in Texas? Now, that would indeed be a *profitable* achievement, certainly. But money is the

Sirens' song that saps our wills. Killing you would hardly be something to be proud of.''

''Oh, I don't know about that,'' Bill said amiably. ''I mean, *I'd* be proud to kill me. I'll take three,'' he added to Josh, who was dealing and listening to the conversation.

But Josh was having trouble concentrating on his task. The barroom was far more crowded this evening, and the nervous reporter anticipated another attack at any moment. By now it was no secret that Wild Bill Hickok was roosting in Progress City. At the bar, the loafers had shed their usual slouches; lidded eyes constantly shifted toward Hickok's table.

''Raise you a dollar,'' Bill said.

''Money in my pocket, Wild Bill, money in my pocket.''

Josh figured that Blackford—Richard Strickland, he corrected himself—must have finally decided he was being too obvious. Tonight, he was not so blatantly sandbagging at poker. He had won several good pots so far. However, Bill still had more poker chips stacked beside his usual bottle of Old Taylor, the bourbon that featured Colonel Edmund Haynes Taylor's signature on each label.

Bill, Josh noticed, looked relaxed and at peace, as he almost always did. But by now the reporter knew Hickok well—the man's lateral vision was constantly monitoring the barroom for trouble. And his back was flat against a wall.

''How's business been going, Mr. Blackford?''

Hickok asked conversationally while he arranged his cards.

The question seemed innocent enough. But as usual, Blackford did not answer immediately. This, Josh realized, was a man who figured percentages and angles. A cautious man who paused even before the simplest of answers, making sure of his own interest first.

"Quite sound, Mr. Hickok, thank our Creator. My company's new line of plumbing fixtures is selling great guns. It's amazing how many folks want a bath-tub right inside their homes nowadays. Prejudices against frequent bathing are finally breaking down. Perhaps someday, Bill, the average American male will be as well-groomed as you are."

Bill inclined his head slightly to acknowledge the compliment. One finger smoothed his neat blond mus-tache while he decided how many discards to throw down.

"Actually, I meant the *railroad* business," Bill said, so casually it almost sounded like an after-thought.

It caught Josh by surprise, too. He watched Black-ford's bland face carefully. For just a moment, the mask finally cracked. But that moment passed in a heartbeat. To buy time, Blackford took a few extra puffs on his pipe. Josh heard spit rattling in the stem.

"The railroad business?" Blackford repeated, po-litely baffled. "Why, I'd imagine it's going just fine, Bill. You'll have to ask a railroad man, though. Not a drummer."

Bill nodded. "Three cards, damnit," he told Josh. Josh slapped them down onto the green baize, his eyes again cutting to the well-armed men crowding the bar.

"I been thinking about this," Johnny Kinkaid told Barry. " 'Course I want Hickok dead. But this ain't how I want it done."

The two men were waiting in Blackford's room. A few minutes earlier, the Chinese kid had stopped by to give them Hickok's room number.

"I don't believe this," Tate objected. "*You're* the one's been arguing full-bore how we need to settle Hickok's hash. Now you get chicken guts?"

Johnny, busy scraping dried mud off his boots on a chair edge, looked a warning at the other man. "You'll ease off that talk, Barry, or you'll wear one of them suits with no back in it."

Barry started pacing the room, his blunt features a mask of hatred. Each time he thought about how Hickok humiliated him at the Peatross place, rage filled him like a bucket under a pump.

"But *why,* Johnny? Christ! We *got* to do for Hickok, or he'll make sure we all cop it."

"I didn't just fall off the hay wagon," Johnny shot back. "I *know* it's important to kill him. But there's an old saying: 'Make a plow horse, but spoil a racer.' "

"You wanna spell that out plain?"

"It's like this," Johnny explained. "Personally, I don't give a damn if you or somebody else murders

Hickok in his damned bed. Dead is dead, and he needs killing. But you got to remember what I am—maybe the fastest draw, and the best aim, inside *or* outside of Bill Cody's troupe."

Despite his foul mood, Barry had to nod agreement here. He'd once seen Wyatt Earp draw down on a gun-sharp in Wichita. Earp was fast, but Johnny Kinkaid was faster.

"All right, then. *I* don't have to dry-gulch Hickok. Why hide my lights under a bushel? I can stare that smirking Irish bastard straight in the eye while I fill his guts with a load of blue whistlers! Hey? Goddamn right I can!"

For all the world to know and respect, Johnny thought. And fear. Bill Hickok was the greatest coup feather in the West. Johnny wanted to wear that feather *openly* like a proud warrior—not slinking around bragging to drunk strangers how he back-shot Hickok from a dark closet.

"All that's air pudding," Barry objected, nervously snapping the wheel of one of his spurs with his finger. "We just need Hickok cold as a wagon wheel, Johnny! Nothing fancy. You yourself been banging our ears about how we're neither up the well nor down, how we got to put the quietus on Hickok quick and be shut of him. He could ruin a fortune for all three of us. He's bound to find out about this Burlington deal."

Johnny's insolent mouth twisted in scorn. "You ain't birding there—he could sink us. But you ain't frettin' no fortune, Tate. For you, this whole shooting match is all about Nell. You can't stand the thought of another man, especially Hickok, eatin' off your plate."

Anger heat washed into Barry's face. But before he could retort, Johnny heaved himself out of the chair and aimed for the door.

"Do what you want to, Barry, I ain't your mama. But I'm telling you, when *I* shoot at Hickok, it'll be face-to-face in a showdown."

"There's a few dozen or so dead men have made that same brag, Johnny."

But Kinkaid had spoken his piece, and now he left. Before he shut the door behind him, he repeated, "Do what you want to. But *don't* queer the deal for all of us."

After Johnny had gone, Barry continued to mull his options while he sipped whiskey from a pony glass. Again he worked himself up to a slow boil, his thoughts rough and ugly as he recalled the galling things Hickok had said to him. Unlike Johnny, Barry knew he could never hope to face Hickok in a fair fight. Which also meant that hiding inside Hickok's room was out of the question.

But perhaps . . .

Barry's slightly glazed eyes cut to his Sharps .50, propped against the nearest wall. Barry was a better shot with a rifle, anyway. Maybe, just maybe, room seven would offer a good line of fire from outside?

Tate descended to the first floor and quickly ascertained that room seven was at the back of the hotel. He returned to the lobby, avoiding the night clerk, and stepped outside into the cool darkness of the spring night. Moments later, hope worked into his face.

The window of room number seven opened onto a service alley behind the hotel!

Tate's horse was hitched to the tie rail in front of the hotel. He moved it around into the alley and hobbled it foreleg to rear, ready to escape in moments. Barry took up a good position behind a stack of wooden packing crates close to Hickok's window.

Barry jacked a round into the chamber. *One good shot*, he told himself. Win, lose, or draw. And then he'd be gone before the echo from his rifle fell silent.

"Hickok's a dead 'un," Barry vowed in the silver-white moonlight.

"Playing poker is the *only* time to count on luck," Wild Bill boasted to his young companion as they strolled the long hallway, returning to their rooms after the card game. "Luck is a lady, Longfellow, and the ladies *like* me, you know that."

Josh couldn't help grinning at this rare side of Bill. He was not, by nature, a boastful man. But tonight he was a little tipsy, and his winnings had made him a bit smug.

"*Never* count on luck," Bill reiterated as he licked his thumb and counted the banknotes in his fist. "Luck is a fickle whore."

The narrow hallway was lighted by gas lights in tin wall sconces. Shadows glided like ghostly predators. Behind one of the doors, Josh heard a man snoring with a racket like a boar hog.

Josh stopped in front of his door, but Bill clapped a hand on his shoulder. "I've got a bottle in my room, kid. Let's have a nightcap and plan our strategy."

When Bill reached room seven, he sobered up considerably. Josh watched him first examine the floor near the door carefully. Then Bill listened with his ear on the door for what seemed like a full minute.

"Safe as sassafras," he finally announced, straightening up and keying the lock.

Bill swung open the door and struck a match on the jamb. He lit a gas lamp on the wall and turned up the flame, pushing shadows back into the corners of the room.

"Damn," Josh heard Bill mutter when he accidentally dropped his winnings.

At the very moment Bill bent down to retrieve his money off the floor, all hell broke loose.

The glass in the sash window shattered inward, and a fist-size chunk of plaster exploded from the wall just about where Bill's head had been a split second earlier. And last, though so close it all came as one racket, came the sharp crack of a rifle.

A moment later, even as the drumbeat of hooves faded outside, Bill came sheepishly to his feet—sheepishly, Josh realized, because the man who "never counted on luck" had just been saved by that "fickle whore."

Bill's sheepishness turned to surprise when he realized *his* guns were both still holstered, while Josh had his out and cocked.

"Well, Longfellow," Bill remarked, fastidiously dusting off the knees of his trousers, "looks like you took a page from my book. Instead of a nightcap, think I'll settle for a slice of humble pie."

Josh crossed to the shattered window and carefully looked out into the grainy darkness. He could see nothing but shadows and shapes, all inanimate.

"He's long gone," Bill remarked, poking a cheroot between his teeth. "Tomorrow we'll cut sign on that horse that just left. I'd wager the trail will lead straight to the Rocking K."

Josh, still facing the window, was about to reply when a vague alarm suddenly tingled the nape of his neck: He whiffed the smell of grain alcohol, rancid body odor, and old bear grease, all combined in one stench.

"Dogs! My men are both alive, praise Jesus!"

Josh spun around on his heel. Wild Bill had become Timid Bill. His eyes those of a panicked doe, Hickok had backed up against the nearest wall. Calamity Jane, a huge, grape-purple bruise swelling one eye shut, stepped into the room and closed the door with her foot.

Jane grinned lecherously, her eyes cutting from one "sweet hunk of manhood" to the other.

"Howdy, boys," she announced. "Can a gal get a drink around here? How 'bout it?"

Chapter Twelve

Fortunately for Hickok, the night clerk found him an empty room after Jane passed out drunk on the floor of number seven, losing consciousness in the middle of screeching a Sioux battle song.

But unfortunately for Hickok, he had to sneak back into room seven early the next morning, at the risk of waking Calamity Jane.

"Give me your pocketknife," Bill whispered to Josh as they tiptoed around the pile where Jane lay sleeping, still fully clothed. "And be quiet."

Josh watched Bill and realized he *wasn't* tiptoeing—he was walking on his heels from old habit as a scout working behind enemy lines. Bill crossed to the place where the rifle slug, fired last night, had thwacked into the wall. Bill dug into the hole with Josh's knife and soon extracted a flattened slug.

They returned to the safety of the hallway.

"It's either a .44 or a .50 caliber," Bill said when they were safely returned to the hallway. "It was made in a bullet mold, not by a factory press. But it's hard to know the caliber exactly once the slug's been knocked out of shape. It's like what you get when you put a nickel on the railroad track—hard to tell it from a dime once it's been flattened."

Bill dropped the slug into his shirt pocket. "C'mon, kid. We'll get some chuck in our bellies, then cut sign on our trigger-happy visitor."

Very little traffic had passed through the alley since the shooting incident the night before. Even city-slicker Josh, who according to Bill "couldn't locate your own ass at high noon in a hall of mirrors," could read the clear signs. One man had waited among the empty packing crates, then fled on horseback through the alley.

Also as Bill had predicted, the ambusher's trail led straight toward Elmer Kinkaid's Rocking K spread. Along the way they encountered a third rider, likewise bearing toward the Rocking K: homesteader Dave Hansen, his big, moon face choleric with rage. The butt plate of his long Henry rifle rested on his right thigh.

"Dave, you 'pear to be loaded for bear," Wild Bill said in greeting.

"Bears I'll abide, by grab! I'm loaded for goddamned, yellow-bellied, back-shooting cow nurses!"

"I take it you're heading for the Rocking K?"

"Yah, shoor! Dirty sons of bitches, I'll—"

''Simmer down, Swede,'' Bill urged him. ''They'll cut you to trap bait! Now, what the hell happened?''

''You got a minute, Bill? It's not far to my place. I show you what the bastards done last night.''

Bill nodded. They jogged left off the stage trail and reached Hansen's quarter-section in fifteen minutes.

''Look,'' Hansen told them, his voice tight with feeling. Unable to look himself, he pointed toward a little fenced-off pasture behind his sod dugout.

Josh followed his finger and could see nothing to shock the eye. Only a magnificent sixteen-hand stallion, a bay with impressive muscle conformation and powerful haunches.

''Only thing I own that's worth a plugged nickel,'' Hansen said.

''Fine-looking stud animal,'' Bill approved. ''He'll sire you a fine line of horseflesh.''

At Bill's remark, Hansen winced as if he'd been slugged.

''Yah,'' Hansen said bitterly. ''Move in closer, gents, and take a good look at him.''

Josh and Bill did. Abruptly Bill sucked in a hissing breath. ''God kiss me,'' he muttered. ''Look, kid.''

Bill pointed, and Josh suddenly curled his toes at the sight. The magnificent stallion had been ''gun castrated''—deliberately shot so he would lose little blood but could never sire again.

''Last night,'' Josh muttered to Bill. ''While we played cards—or while we arm-wrestled with Jane.''

''You'll whip her next time,'' Bill consoled his friend before he turned back to Hansen.

"See how it is?" Hansen demanded. "I had a horse get caught in bobwire before. Legs sliced so bad I had to shoot it. But *this*—just cold and deliberate-like."

"You see who did it?"

"Nuh-uh. But the tracks lead to Elmer Kinkaid's spread."

Hansen picked up a rock and flung it hard, so angry he had to do something. When he spoke, his voice was balanced between rage and despair. "What are us homesteaders supposed to *do*, Wild Bill? Back east, why hell! The damned manufactories is takin' the trade from skilled workers. My papa was a master shoemaker, and he taught me his trade. But I can't cut leather half so cheap as the 'factories. Don't matter, I reckon. Looks like I'll be pulling stakes, going back east to work in a factory or a meat plant with the rest of the wage slaves."

"You got better leather in you than that," Bill told the despondent man. "Hansen, you're tough as a grizz! It was sodbusters like you won the Civil War while all those 'hunters and adventurers' from the West deserted after their first battle. You ain't been run out yet. If I told you the worst is over for you, wouldja stay—and fight, if it comes to that?"

Hansen studied the dapper gunslinger. "If *you* say so, yah shoor."

"Well, I do say so. It's a long lane that has no turning, my friend. Things around here will soon come to a head, you got my word on it. That's my specialty—stirring up the mud."

Bill swung up and over, reining his horse around. "C'mon, kid. Let's dust our hocks toward Elmer's place."

It was Nell Kinkaid who answered their knock, looking pretty and feminine in a navy blue dress with velvet-trimmed cuffs.

"Why, Mr. Hickok," she said with mock surprise. "I didn't expect you to actually *knock*!"

Bill grinned, realizing she was alluding to his untimely interruption, last visit, of her bath.

"It's good to see you again, Nell. Even if I do see *less* this time."

Josh watched Nell's polished-apple cheeks blush even deeper. "I hope you were pleased with what you saw," she said softly as both men removed their hats and stepped inside.

"The demonstration was appealing," Bill assured her. "Now I'd like to sample the wares."

Nell's dark eyes flashed indignation at this boldness. But before she could retort, Elmer Kinkaid wheeled his chair into the room and greeted both men. Josh saw the walnut gun stock in his lap. By now it was stained and sealed with linseed oil, a handsome piece of work.

"Well, boys! What's the good word?"

"Attempted murder," Bill replied, taking the flattened rifle slug out of his pocket. "Somebody tried to kill me last night, which isn't exactly a remarkable event for me. But I followed the shooter's back trail to the Rocking K."

Elmer's deep-seamed face frowned. He took the slug and examined it. "Here you go again, Wild Bill. The cattlemen hired you to get the homesteaders off our backs. So here you are, pointing the finger at the cowmen again."

"I just cut wood," Bill replied stubbornly, "and let the chips fall where they may."

Elmer twisted a finger into his shaggy white mustache, mulling this.

"Well, damnit," the old patriarch told the world in general. Then he expelled a long, fluming sigh. "I trust you, Bill. You *sure* the trail led here?"

"Sure as cats fighting," Bill said. "Is Barry Tate around?"

Nell had been listening to all this in attentive silence. Now Josh saw her and Elmer both start at this question.

"Barry's rounding up yearling calves near Cheyenne Valley," Elmer said. "Won't be back all day."

"How 'bout your son, Johnny?"

Josh expected the old man to boil over at the question. Instead, he only gazed stoically out the window into the middle distance, his eyes thoughtful. He's been thinking about things since our last visit, Josh realized.

"Johnny's gone, too," Elmer finally replied, his tone speculative. "Matter of fact, he rode out just about the time you two were riding in."

"Almost as if," Nell put in, "he doesn't want to meet you for some reason."

Bill nodded. Nell's remark was innocent enough.

But it made sense to Josh. Johnny Kinkaid was some pumpkins with a gun. If a proud man like that planned on killing another man, he'd hardly want to shake his hand and exchange pleasantries with him.

"Elmer," Bill said, "would Barry take his long gun with him to work cattle?"

Elmer shook his hoary head. "Naw. No cowboy would unless there was rustlers or Injuns afoot. A long gun gets in the way when you dally rope. You take just your short gun to kill snakes 'n' such."

"That's what I figured. Will you come out to the bunkhouse with me? I want to look at Barry's rifle."

Old man Kinkaid, Josh could tell, was damned unhappy about the turn this trail was taking. But the cattle baron was a genuine "God fearer," as they were called on the frontier: men who seldom went to church, but read their Scriptures and read them well. Bill called them "Christian soldiers who cuss."

Elmer nodded. "Let's get it done, then."

Elmer used a special wooden ramp to roll down off the porch. Then Josh pushed his chair across the hoof-packed main yard toward a split-slab bunkhouse behind the breaking corral. The bunkhouse was deserted except for a few night-riding cattle guards, all snoring like threshers. The place had a grim masculine smell of sweat, leather, tobacco, and horse liniment.

As the ramrod, Barry had a separate room at the head of the bunkhouse.

"That's Barry's long gun," Elmer said, pointing to a weapon in a buckskin sheath, balanced on a pair of wall pegs. "Sharps .50. I bought it for him myself to reward the man for five years of steady service to the Rocking K. He's a top hand with cattle."

Bill lifted down the rifle, unsheathed it, and removed a bullet from the fourteen-shot ammo well. Josh watched him pull the lead slug from the cartridge with his teeth.

"Made in a mold," Bill noted, comparing the fresh slug with the spent one, holding both in his palm. Josh could tell they were the same general type of slug.

"It's not proof," Wild Bill conceded. "But it could well have come from this same rifle. There's almost a dozen different types of slug that rifle could take. And this kind, with the dimpled tip, ain't common."

Elmer, Josh noticed, had fallen into a gloomy depression. "This ain't no proof, Hickok," he snapped.

"I just said that, Elmer."

"So what's your next play?"

Bill looked at Josh. "Me and the Philadelphia Kid here are going to take a ride over to Turk's Creek."

"The hell for? Bill, that's good water, all right. But it's no use to me or any other rancher in this territory. Since you've obviously got your bead sighted on the cattlemen, why poke through *those* diggings?"

"Elmer, my bead ain't sighted nowhere. I'm plinking at targets of opportunity."

Elmer grinned at that one, though begrudgingly. "Whatever pops up, uh?"

Bill grinned back. "Straight words, old-timer. One trail led me out here. Another trail—a *paper* trail at the land office—leads to Turk's Creek."

Josh had been waiting for Bill to ask the old settler

about Hansen's mutilated stallion. But Hickok evidently believed Elmer already had enough to stew on.

"Let's grab leather, kid," Bill told Josh quietly. They left Elmer alone in the bunkhouse, his gray features a mask of worry and troubled reflection.

"The old man's taking it hard," Wild Bill remarked as the two riders were circling Dave Hansen's farm. "But he's got me over a barrel on one point. I can't see any link between Turk's Creek and this so-called county war. Near as I can see, there's no reason for cattlemen to care if farmers like Hansen run mother ditches off a creek nobody else can use."

"And if it's the Burlington wants it," Josh threw in, thinking of Jarvis Blackford, "what for? Boiler water, maybe. Except there's plenty of other creeks around here. We've crossed dozens in the last few days."

"That's the way of it, kid," Bill agreed, his sun-slitted eyes scanning the terrain. "Poser, ain't it?"

Josh studied the map Pinkerton gave them, holding it pressed against his saddle horn. Bill had no deadline for solving his case, but Josh had an impatient editor in New York City who was clamoring for more Wild Bill stories.

They were crossing a low rise, still three miles northwest of Turk's Creek, when the hawk-eyed Hickok cut into his thoughts.

"Speaking of the Burlington, glom what's up ahead, Longfellow."

Josh had to look for a long time before he spotted

it: a low pile of rocks with a short stake, lettered and numbered, protruding from it.

"Railroad marker," Bill explained.

Now Josh could see a long line of the survey stakes snaking out across the low, grassy hills. "They're going away from Turk's Creek," Josh pointed out.

Bill nodded. Despite the coincidence of having just mentioned the railroad, he didn't seem particularly surprised by this discovery—nor should he, Josh realized. The West was currently rife with various railroad-construction projects. The transcontinental railroad had linked up at Promontory, Utah, only a few years earlier. And that was only one line—a half-dozen more were now establishing their own east–west links.

Nonetheless, Bill said, "Let's follow the stakes awhile. Turk's Creek ain't going nowhere soon."

Before long a work crew edged into view. Josh saw they were clearing out a stretch of gnarled cottonwood trees. The trees had already been felled. Now workers were drilling holes under the stumps with posthole augers, planting powder charges.

Well ahead of the work crew, a surveyor was measuring ground with a Gunter's chain. Closer to the first work crew, grader operators swore at their mules as they scraped the highest ground lower and pushed the fill into the hollows.

"I've scouted for a few construction crews," Bill told Josh. "It's always the same process. First the line is sighted through by a survey team. Then come the tree sweepers, the graders, the roadbed crew, the track layers. This project just got started—there's no ties or rails stacked up yet.''

Bill spotted the gang boss, a big, florid-faced Irishman in twill coveralls who introduced himself as Big Sandy O'Hara. At first he scowled at the new arrivals, too busy to deal with gawkers.

But Wild Bill Hickok was a bona fide railroad legend by now, having protected dozens of track crews in hostile Indian country. The moment Big Sandy learned Bill's identity, he broke out a bottle of Old Taylor—Wild Bill's brand had become the brand of America's railmen.

''We're punching a spur line south to Laramie,'' Big Sandy explained. ''It'll save the area cattlemen a world of time and money and trouble. Now they won't have to drive cattle to the Laramie railhead.''

As the two riders were moving on again, Big Sandy called out to Josh, ''Hey, kid? Need a job?''

The gang boss pointed to the surveyor. ''Tommy needs a man to hold the sticks for him. Boring, but it pays good.''

Josh waved his no thanks, and the two men covered the stretch to Turk's Creek in silence, each alone with his thoughts. As Bill had predicted, there was little to see once they arrived.

Turk's Creek was actually a small river. Nothing distinguished it except the fact that it was exceptionally clear and sandy-bottomed.

''Looks a lot like the Niobrara in the Nebraska panhandle country,'' Wild Bill remarked thoughtfully, studying the crystal-clear water while their horses tanked up. But soon buffalo gnats swarmed their faces, and the two men began their ride back to Progress City.

"Bill, what's going on around here?" Josh demanded at one point, interrupting a long silence.

Instead of brushing the question off as he usually did, Wild Bill actually drew rein and sat his saddle for a full minute, pondering it.

"Kid, do you recall how I told you to scout? How you actually *look* at open terrain?"

Josh nodded. "You said—you said a man has to avoid sending his eye out to seize one image. Instead, he has to let *all* the images come up to his eye. Then he can pick out the ones that matter."

Bill nodded, pleased with his young friend's memory for survival details. "That's good, kid. You nailed it solid. Now see, I think we've already *looked* at the answer to your question, y'unnerstan'?"

Josh felt his scalp tingle at the depth of Bill's insight.

"Sure," the youth replied. "The answer's been here all along. Now all we got to do is pick it out."

"That's it." Bill whistled at his roan, kicking him forward again. "And try to stay alive until we can do it."

Chapter Thirteen

Quite reluctantly, Wild Bill moved out of the relative comfort of the Medicine Bow Hotel early the next morning. Grumbling about the primitive amenities, Hickok set up residence in a deserted soddy north of Progress City.

Bill made this decision, he informed Josh, after he'd made a trip to the rickety jakes and bathhouse out behind the hotel. Something about the way that skinny Chinese kid with the carbuncle on his neck watched him, Bill explained, made him uneasy—there was *guilt* in that look.

Naturally Josh insisted on going with Bill. Hickok reminded the kid he came west to *report* the news, not be a part of it. But Josh said it was too late for that. Besides, he added, Wild Bill *was* the news, and didn't Josh have to go where the story went? Josh finally settled things in his favor by reminding Bill he'd have a good cook along. Hickok would perform any mundane tasks he had to, but if he could exploit others to do them, all the better.

"By the way, kid," Bill remarked dryly while the two companions finished a simple but plentiful supper of beans and bacon, "I read the latest dispatch you filed by telegraph. I oughta take a switch to your young ass!"

Josh, busy scouring out his mess kit with sand in front of the soddy, grinned wickedly. He had predicted the pithy lead to his story, about the latest attempt on Bill's life, would ruffle Hickok's feathers.

" 'Wild Bill Hickok has a new love,' " Bill quoted sarcastically. " 'And her name is Lady Luck.' That's a pile of crap!"

"Then what else saved you?" Josh demanded. "If you hadn't bent over to pick up your winnings, you'd've caught a bullet between the eyes."

"Kid," Hickok fumed, "*this* is why I like Ned Buntline. *He* would've claimed I deliberately dropped that money, woulda turned it into a clever trick, see?"

"Lied, right?"

"Ahh . . . what's the difference? You girls who scribble for publication don't know your ass from your elbow anyhow! Just like in all those dime novels you've got in your saddlebags: The bad guy is always safe once he races across the border into Mexico. What a crock! You been to Mex? That country is so lawless, any man with boots or a horse is shot on sight."

Bill fell silent, and Josh heard the wind rippling through the rolling sea of buffalo grass surrounding them. The deserted sod house—legacy of a homesteader who pulled up stakes—was built against a low hill and offered an excellent view of the territory in all directions. The two men had fixed and eaten their supper outside—inside, the soddy was musty with the dank stink of roots growing down from the ceiling.

Nearby, Bill's roan and Josh's little blue were chomping grass on long tethers. It had been broad daylight when Josh dug the firepit. But now, even as he watched, the sun didn't really set—it just suddenly seemed to collapse, and abruptly it was night.

"What's the plan now, Bill?" Josh asked.

"Nothing mail-order, that's for sure. Just old-fashioned nose-to-the-wind stuff. Since everything seems to happen at night around here lately, I figure *we* should become night riders, too. So tonight we patrol. Wear dark clothes, and make sure you strap on your short iron before we ride out."

"Patrol where?"

Bill shrugged, spilling the dregs of his coffee into the grass. "Where else? We ain't in China, kid! The farms, the ranches, just patrolling the country hereabouts. A man can't conquer the world from his front yard."

They set out soon afterward. Moonlight was generous on the open flats and visibility was good. But under the trees it was darker than the inside of a boot. The land they rode through was mostly gullies, bottom woods, and grass, with the occasional timbered sidehills, runoff seams carved into them.

As the moon inched toward its zenith, the two men held their well-rested animals to a steady trot, both to conserve their strength and to minimize noise. Now and then Josh heard an owl hoot or the far-off, eerie roar of a puma's kill cry. But so far, the Wyoming night seemed peaceful enough.

"Quiet, ain't it?" Josh remarked at one point.

"Sure is," Bill replied. "And so is a fish on ice, if you take my meaning?"

Josh took it, all right. Wild Bill had his own way of making a point. Josh forced his mind to quit daydreaming and rested his right palm on the butt of his pistol.

"We got serious troubles now," Johnny Kinkaid said urgently. "Mack and Stoney were hazing strays east of my old man's land yesterday. They saw Hickok jawing with the Burlington work crew. Won't be long now, he'll twig our game. I knew that son of a bitch was a fast draw. Nobody warned me he's got a full brainpan, too."

With Hickok somewhere out there on the prowl, the three conspirators had met in Blackford's hotel room instead of the deserted line shack.

"Actually," Blackford remarked conversationally, tamping tobacco into his pipe, "you won't hear of *any* true marksmen who are stupid. Wyatt Earp, John Wesley Hardin, Bat Masterson—superior reflexes must be controlled by a superior intellect, or—"

"Who gives a damn?" Barry Tate snapped impatiently. "You're always talking like a book. We don't need a damn schoolmaster."

"Now, now," Jarvis goaded. "It wasn't my talking like a book that ruined your point-blank shot at Hickok, was it?"

Barry's face twitched, but he said nothing. Jarvis looked at Johnny.

"As far as Hickok talking to the work crew—remember, Johnny, these rail-gang workers don't know anything, yet, about the problem with the hard water in Kinkaid County. Hickok can't have any good reason to link that construction with us."

All three men fervently hoped so, anyway. Despite the fact that Kinkaid County was crisscrossed by creeks, streams, and rivers, much of it was some of the most mineral-rich water in the West. So "hard" with minerals, in fact, that one government agriculturalist quipped it was "solid water." This hard water was fine for most purposes, but the railroads had only recently realized that mineral-rich water quickly reduced the capacity of cast-iron boilers by gumming the steam vents with semisolid mineral deposits.

Thus, the Burlington's current spur-line project hinged on one important condition: Since Kinkaid County was the optimal location for an important water-storage station, the water rights to Turk's Creek—the only "soft" water in that area—and much of the surrounding land must be sold to the railroad. Most of the land titles to that area were already in Johnny and Barry's names—Dave Hansen and a couple of other homesteaders were the last holdouts. And they would never sell cheap, which meant driving them out—and creating a reason to do so.

"Keeping it dark from Hickok," Blackford added, "is fairly easy so long as Hickok doesn't suspect who's really killing the cows around here. Remember, the feeder ditch hasn't yet been dug to Turk's Creek. It's so far away, no one connects the creek to the Burlington project."

"Has their money offer been firmed up?" Johnny demanded.

Blackford nodded. "Firm as granite. Gentlemen, we're looking at the figure of a hundred thousand dollars."

This revelation forced a respectful silence. That meant more than $33,000 apiece—at a time when a top hand on a ranch made only $360 *per year*. For Johnny, that meant he could pay his poker debts and still be twenty thousand to the good.

"But we're also," Blackford cautioned, "looking at the growing problem of Wild Bill Hickok."

Johnny and Barry exchanged a glance. Johnny flashed his insolent grin and pulled a perfumed sheet of folded stationery from his shirt pocket.

"Me and Barry have been working on that problem," Johnny said. "And we've got a good plan. We can use my sister Nell as bait to set Hickok up for the trap. You know how Hickok can't say no to a pert woman? Well, I had Dottie McGratten, that soldier's widow, write this note out and sign Nell's name. She splashed toilet water all over it, too. It'll put Hickok in rut quick. I'm told he's left the hotel, but he's still picking up messages there.''

Blackford unfolded the note. It was written in blue ink, an ornate feminine hand:

Dear Wild Bill,
We never get a chance to be alone at my home. Are you as unhappy about this fact as I am? If so, why not meet me day after tomorrow, around noon, where the stage road intersects with the Old Evansville Pike two miles west of town.
Nell Kinkaid

Blackford grinned and looked at both men, admiration clear in his eyes. ''That'll fetch him, all right. It's red meat to a starving hound! But how do you guarantee your sister will be where the note says? Surely she's not in cahoots with you?''

Johnny snorted at the very idea. ''Nell? Shoo! If she ever broke a law, she'd wear ashes and sackcloth for a year, the Little Miss Goody. See, the deal is, Nell really will be passing that spot around noon—she's got an appointment with Holly Nearhood, the seamstress, to pick up a dress Holly altered for her. And Nell will be on time. I heard her whine to my pa how tight Holly's schedule always is.''

''Hickok's no fool,'' Tate threw in. ''The letter will get him all het up, all right. But he'll be suspicious, that's his nature. He won't show himself until he's sure Nell is alone and not being followed. Then he'll ride down to meet her. And it's all open right there at that intersection—a man who takes up a good position an hour or so earlier will get one clean shot.''

''It *won't* be me,'' Johnny said before Jarvis could ask. ''I'll go along. And if something goes bad, I'll kill Hickok *if* it can be face-to-face. But I want Barry to plug him. That miss in town was a fluke. Barry is only so-so with his short gun. But with a rifle, he can drop a man at two hundred yards every shot.''

''And we've already scouted out that spot,'' Barry said. ''I can easily hide within fifty yards.''

Blackford looked at each man in turn. ''It's a good plan. Johnny, didn't I tell you good shootists are clever? But don't forget. Your sister will be a witness.''

''To what?'' Johnny demanded. ''Hickok dying, is all. Barry won't have to show. And if I show, it'll only be for a fair gunfight. I *want* her to see that.''

Jarvis tapped the dottle out of his pipe, looking well satisfied. ''Gents, I've raised my final objection. Good luck. Next time we meet, here's hoping we can drink to Wild Bill Hickok's memory.''

Josh and Wild Bill had been riding in the darkness for hours. Long enough for Bill to go through two entire cheroots, and he was one to savor a slow cigar. So far the night seemed uneventful. By now Josh felt cold slicing at his neck, and he turned up his collar.

''Let's see what you're learning, kid,'' Bill said as they stopped to spell their horses in a big clearing carved out by lightning. ''What time is it?''

Both of them owned watches. But Josh left his in

his pocket and glanced up at the fat ball of moon. Bill had taught him to tell approximate time by it: It was pure white early at night, and turned more golden as the night advanced.

"Heading up toward four A.M.," Josh guessed. "Maybe a little past."

Bill thumbed back the cover of his watch. "Kid, you must be a descendant of Daniel Boone! It's four-fifteen."

Josh felt a tight bubble of pride. Bill only had to show or tell him a thing once, and it was his for life. But then again, there was an awful lot a man had to learn. Even the quickest study could easily die before he learned enough.

"Let's take one last look at Hansen's place," Bill decided. "Then we'll turn in for a few hours."

They picked up the course of Turk's Creek and followed it toward Hansen's farm. Bill kept them on low ground as much as possible to avoid the skyline.

Just below the crest of a low ridge overlooking Hansen's place, Wild Bill suddenly halted. Josh reined in, too.

"S'matter?" Josh hissed.

"Look at the treeline left of Dave's place. Watch it from the side of your eye."

Josh did. Soon he thought he could make out a shadowy human form hidden there.

"C'mon," Bill whispered, quickly dismounting and hobbling his roan.

Josh followed Bill's example, walking on his heels to minimize ground contact. He also drew his pinfire revolver when he saw Bill slide one of his Peacemakers out of its holster.

When they were within fifteen feet of the hidden intruder, Bill thumbed back the hammer. Its click sounded ominous in the quiet night air.

"There's two guns aimed at you, mister," Bill called out. "Back out of there slow, slow as molasses in January. Then drop your weapon *before* you turn around. Do it just like I told you. One mistake, and tonight you'll cross the Great Divide."

"Christ, mister, don't shoot!" pleaded a familiar voice. Josh heard an ungodly rattling and thrashing and shaking of bushes, as if a longhorn were caught there. A huge man backed out and dropped his Winchester to the ground. He turned around. Josh recognized Sheriff Waldo, a typhoid tinge to his skin in the ghostly moonlight.

"My apologies, Sheriff," Bill said, holstering his gun. He looked at the spyglass Waldo still held in his left hand. "Doing some nighttime work, eh?"

"Ahh, tryin' to do what I can, Bill. You boys coming to see me, that put a little fire under me. I been sittin' on my fat ass too long now, Bill. Hell, look what *you* done as sheriff in Hays City and Abilene."

Josh could tell from the self-loathing in Waldo's tone that the man was suffering from guilt.

"I did all right," Bill agreed. "But I was paid a hundred and fifty dollars a month to get it done."

Sheriff Waldo snorted. "Well, I don't draw near *that* kind of pay. But it's still high time I earned what I do get. Bill, you seen all them wanted dodgers in my office? You know what I do with 'em?"

Bill laughed. "Sure I do. I was a starman, too, and did the same thing. You use 'em for kindling in the winter, don'tcha?"

Waldo laughed right back. "Even you?"

"Hell, every sheriff does. Well, seen any signs of trouble tonight, Sheriff?"

"It's been quiet as a country grave. How 'bout you?"

"The same, old son, the same. Makes me nervous. Well, keep up the good work."

"I plan to," Sheriff Waldo assured them. "Can't every man be a Bill Hickok, but I can do better than I been doing. And by God, I will."

Josh watched Bill reach out and give the big man a hearty handshake. "Any man who does his best can rest easy. Good luck to you, Sheriff. Let's keep in touch on what we find."

"You bet, Wild Bill!"

The two friends left the newly reformed Sheriff Waldo at his hidden observation post. Not once did Josh suspect that, next time they laid eyes on Waldo, he'd be stone-cold dead.

Chapter Fourteen

Early on the second day after discovering Sheriff Waldo on night patrol, Wild Bill and Josh rode into Progress City to run some errands.

Josh needed to telegraph his latest offering to his editor at the *Herald*, and Bill needed to check for messages at the hotel as well as pick up some smokes and a bottle of Old Taylor. "A man can cut a new wick out of his long johns," Bill assured Josh. "But there's no substitute for Colonel Taylor."

As always, Hickok's eyes missed little as the two riders trotted into town from the direction of the rolling hills to the west.

"New construction," Josh remarked needlessly, for Bill had already seen it. Both men watched a work gang nailing up boards a quarter-mile south of town.

"Cattle-loading corrals," Bill replied. "That's

about where the Burlington spur line will cut through. Doesn't need to come directly into town, because it's mostly for cow trains.''

Josh could tell from Bill's tone that he was still trying to find a good connection between the spur line and distant Turk's Creek. There was plenty of water closer to hand, including some nobody had yet bothered to claim. So why were Johnny Kinkaid and Barry Tate so obviously grabbing up the land sections around distant Turk's Creek?

The town was just stirring to life for the day. A thin, bald-headed man in a dirty apron looked up from sweeping the boardwalk in front of the mercantile store. He stared at the riders for a long time before deciding to nod. As usual, the forgeman was clearly visible in the big, open doorway of his shop. He was busy rasping the hoofs of a pony smooth, preparing to shoe it.

The hotel seemed nearly deserted. Two old men played checkers in the lobby, spitting at the cuspidor behind the door and missing it more often than they hit it.

''Morning, Wild Bill,'' Jed Rault greeted the famous frontiersman. ''Message for you.'' The hotel clerk added a knowing wink. ''Judging from the smell coming off it, the author is of the female-type persuasion.''

Bill actually winced as he took the envelope, the perfume smell was so powerful. ''Definitely female,'' Bill repeated. ''But she pours on the cologne like a soiled dove, not a Jenny Lind.''

Josh deftly ignored Bill's maneuvering, elbowing in close and reading the note over Bill's shoulder. The reporter couldn't help a little sting of anger—and jealousy—as he read Nell Kinkaid's bold and suggestive note.

Why, in Philadelphia it would be a scandal! So what if Bill *was* famous and handsome and all that? Did that mean that women had to ignore everybody else? Just turn into *his* concubines when Hickok came to town? But in his heart of envious hearts, Josh had to admit: If *he* had received that note, not Bill, he'd be calling Nell "spirited," not a painted woman!

Wild Bill, however, hardly seemed elated by the note.

"Who left this?" he asked Jed.

The clerk grinned. "You think whoever she was wanted *me* to know? This ain't New Orleans, brother! I just found it on the counter."

"Mmm" was all Bill said, reading the note again. "C'mon, Longfellow," he added absently. "Let's send off your latest batch of lies to the crapsheets. Seems I've got an appointment to keep in a few hours."

"Can I go, too?" Josh demanded.

Bill snorted. "What? You like to watch, do you?"

Josh hung fire for a few seconds, not understanding. Then he flushed beet red. Bill laughed so hard, he had to pull his cigar out of his teeth. "Ahh, I'm just playing the larks with you, kid."

Bill's smile lingered. But all mirth suddenly deserted his eyes. "I'll go alone. That note might be from Nell, all right. She's bold enough. But seems to me, Nell's the kind wouldn't *dip* a letter in perfume—she'd give it a trace, not slap you in the face with it. Let's move it, kid. We're burning daylight."

On the ride back to the deserted soddy, Wild Bill lapsed into a long, thoughtful silence. Although Hickok hadn't said much about it, Josh suspected he was thinking more and more about Barry Tate. But even more, Wild Bill was fretting about Johnny Kinkaid.

There's a hole in him somewhere, Elmer had admitted about his son. Bill's concern wasn't just because Johnny was a top hand with a gun—Josh knew Wild Bill better than that by now. Hickok wasn't scared. Wild Bill seldom faced danger in his imagination. Bill had already called that a sure way for a man to turn himself into a coward and ruin life's peaceful moments.

No. Josh knew Bill was worried about Elmer, not Johnny. Bill liked the crusty but decent old man. Just as he liked Waldo, even though the feckless loser was poor shakes as a sheriff.

Bill Hickok liked an odd assortment of persons, with special fondness for the decent underdogs of society. Bill knew that Elmer loved his only son, warts and all. Yet Bill seemed almost certain by now that Johnny Kinkaid was pushing toward a showdown with him. That arrogant punk would be no loss to anyone but Elmer.

The two riders were crossing a stretch where Russian thistle abounded in the low elevations while centuries of hard winds had polished the knolls bare higher up.

"Bill!" Josh warned, suddenly drawing rein. "Eyes left!"

Ahead and below, a gaudy buckboard with painted sideboards blocked the old stage road.

"Katy Christ!" Bill swore. Josh watched his face drain just as Pickett's must have before his ill-fated charge at Gettysburg. Bill glanced desperately around, seeking immediate cover. "It's Calamity Jane. She'll be looking for me," Bill added grimly.

Hickok stared at the grinning kid. "Looking for *you*, too, slim britches! Two men ain't even a side dish for Jane when the appetite is on her."

Hearing this, Josh lost his smug grin. "There's a cutbank to our right," he suggested. "We could cover down before she spots us."

But by now Wild Bill had realized that Jane's wagon had broken down.

"Oh, hell, it's no use! She's sprung an axle, Longfellow. See it trailing? She's trying to reseat it by herself, but she needs a ratchet jack—or some strong arms to help her."

Josh started to protest.

"Bite the bullet, kid," Bill cut him off. "She's coyote ugly and smells like a bear's cave, but how many times has she put her bacon in the fire for us?"

Josh pressured his horse with both knees and followed Bill down the slope. But still he complained. "Man alive, Bill! Don't you *ever* relax your code?"

Bill grinned, liking that. "Nope," he answered cheerfully. "It wouldn't be a code then. It'd be an Indian treaty!" Bill ground his cheroot out on the saddle horn and pocketed the long butt. "C'mon! Hah! Gee up, there!"

But destiny, Josh wrote later in his next wire story, had different plans for them that day. Jane never spotted them, and they never reached her. Because halfway down the long slope, Wild Bill glimpsed something else in the corner of his eye—something, experience told him, that wasn't right.

He reined in, staring toward a copse of box elders and willows on their right. Josh followed his penetrating gaze and saw a saddled horse, minus its rider. He didn't recognize the horse. But the sight didn't strike the youth as particularly sinister.

Nonetheless, Bill said in a tone heavy with foreboding, "Kid, a horse is a naturally curious animal. It likes to look around. You see one with his head down, like that one, he's either ailing or someone has pitched feed. *That* animal ain't eating. C'mon."

The horse stood in the middle of a little cup-shaped hollow. Josh heard the obscene buzzing of bluebottle flies as they drew nearer through the scattering of trees. Then he saw why the horse was ailing: Crusted blood covered its belly like a plaster. Even from here, Josh could see the puckered flesh of a bullet wound.

But a curse from Bill focused Josh's attention square on the real horror: About twenty feet beyond the dying horse, Sheriff Waldo lay murdered.

"That bullet in his back," Hickok said, squatting

near the massive corpse and pointing, "didn't kill him. Knocked him off his wounded horse. He tried to run for it. The killer rode him down like game and did *that*."

Bill nodded at the pebbly mess where the top of Waldo's head had been lifted off like the lid of a cookie jar.

"Point blank with a rifle," Bill added.

It was Wild Bill's quiet tone that alerted Josh to the true depth of Hickok's anger at this cold-blooded killing. For all his limitations, Sheriff Waldo had been a man of conscience in a heartless country. That rated aces high with Wild Bill Hickok. It was going to go hard, Josh predicted, for whoever killed him.

Nell Kinkaid was no coward. She had survived spooked horses, gully washers, stampedes, killer twisters, and rattlesnakes. But she couldn't help a little inner tickle of nervousness as her fringed surrey rolled east along the old stage road that bisected Kinkaid County. Rumor had it the local Indians were out again, having jumped the rez in anger over yet another cut in their government rations.

A clean linen sheet lay folded on the seat beside Nell. The dust hereabouts was already awful, even this early in spring. Nell meant to wrap up her dress, after she picked it up at Holly Nearhood's place, to protect it from the dust on the ride home.

It was the most gorgeous dress in the world! Organdy and tulle, shipped all the way from Paris, France, special order. A dress as elegant and fancy and fine as *any* of Hickok's famous ladies had ever owned. Just *wait* until Wild Bill saw her wearing it!

The trail entered a long, blind turn with steep banks of thornbushes towering high on both sides. The pleasant smile faded from Nell's lips. She flicked at the horse's glossy rump with a light sisal whip, hurrying the animal along.

Barry Tate had taken up an excellent position in a natural nest of rocks. From here, he could see the entire countryside as it rolled up to a pinnacle where the stage road intersected with Old Evansville Pike.

He had smoked the sights of his Sharps .50 to cut reflection when he aimed in this glaring sunlight. Barry still wasn't sure exactly how he missed Hickok when he fired on him through the hotel-room window. Maybe, in his eagerness, he bucked his gun a fraction of an inch.

Whatever. But Barry was damned if that was going to happen again. He had found an opening between two boulders and erected sturdy cross-sticks. Now he could lay the muzzle of the Sharps down steady as a brick on mortar.

Barry wondered idly if anyone had yet discovered Waldo's body. Barry hadn't been looking to kill the meddling sheriff. But the fat fool had revealed his hiding place while Johnny and Barry were poisoning cattle. So Barry had cut him down. Served the dirty traitor right for turning on the cattlemen.

Waldo not only bit the hand that fed him—but he jumped ship to help an outsider, a skirt-chasing gun-slick, at that. Hickok not only believed he could kill whomever he chose—but that he could bed any man's wench, like some godlike feudal landlord, and no man could say anything about it.

"Well, mister, we'll see about *that*," Barry said in a voice just above a whisper.

Finally, after a long and boring wait in his hiding place, Barry heard it: the rattle of tug chains as a conveyance approached the intersection below.

There was Nell! Just now easing out of that long bend around Turkey Tail Mountain. Her sun bonnet was a bright white speck from up here. She'd reach the intersection, Barry estimated, in about five minutes. So *where* in the hell was Hickok?

Barry forced himself to relax, willed his nerves and his breathing steady. He eased his finger inside the trigger guard, ready to take up the slack the moment he found his target.

Just before noon, Wild Bill picketed his roan well off the stage road in a bracken of ferns. He approached the intersection on foot, trying not to break cover. But he could move in only so close before the trees and bushes thinned to open dust flats, vulnerable to any marksmen above.

Bill did not expect trouble. At least, no more trouble than he usually expected. While it was true this was a good ambush spot, it was also a logical place to meet someone. And now Hickok relaxed even more when he spotted Nell Kinkaid, alone in her surrey. If the note was forged in her name, why was she here right on time?

As Nell's conveyance rattled over a plank bridge, Wild Bill stepped out from behind the chokecherry bushes where he'd been hiding. He removed his hat and waved at her with it.

That's when all of it happened, so fast it was over in seconds. But it seemed to take extra long to Bill. Only later was Hickok able to sort out the deadly sequence of events.

The first clue was Nell's reaction upon seeing him. Her smile was genuine, all right. But so was the *surprise* in her eyes. As if, Bill realized in a heartbeat, meeting him was completely unexpected.

"Nell!" Bill roared out. "Stop there and cover down!"

Even before he finished speaking, the first shot from above tagged Bill's left shoulder. It would have nailed him between the shoulder blades, however, had he not already leaped aside.

Nell screamed, the horse reared in its traces, and Bill was scrambling to save his hide. That first bullet had passed through his shoulder clean, causing more heat than pain. But now the shots came rapid as drumbeats. Bill rolled desperately across the trail, just inches ahead of each impacting bullet.

If that was Tate up there, Bill realized desperately, he had fourteen shots in that rifle of his. And Bill was running out of room to outmaneuver them.

Even as he scrambled, however, Wild Bill's trained eyes were looking for target markers. And now he caught a sun glint up above in the corner of his vision. It could easily have been a speck of reflecting quartz or mica. Lacking anything better to shoot at, however, Wild Bill began busting caps at it.

Each time he rolled onto his back, Bill squeezed off a shot toward the rocks and the reflection. At his third close-spaced shot, he heard a man grunt hard. A rifle came crashing and bouncing down the rocky bank, a human body right behind it.

Barry Tate, dead as King David, thumped hard into the trail just in front of Nell and sprawled on his back, his rock-battered, wide-eyed face staring up at her in a grinning death rictus. Nell was so utterly shocked and horrified that she never even bothered to scream—she simply fainted dead away on the spot.

Chapter Fifteen

Wild Bill took a minute to scan the rimrock, making sure no other marksmen were waiting. Then, wincing at a sudden pulse of pain in his shoulder, he hurried around to the driver's side of the surrey. He loosened Nell's high-buttoned collar and gently cuffed her cheeks back to some semblance of their rosy hue.

Nell's thick-curving lashes twitched open. A moment later, realizing that Wild Bill was bleeding, she sat up and gasped audibly.

"Oh, good heart of God! You've been *hit,* Bill!"

"Just winged me," Bill said modestly but truthfully. As far as combat wounds went, he knew this one was piddling. The bullet passed harmlessly through flesh just beneath the shoulder bone. Bill had carbolic acid in his saddlebag, and he'd pour some of that into it. Carbolic got him through several wounds during the war.

But Nell sucked in a hissing breath when she tugged Bill's shirt away. The way blood had streamed all over Hickok's left pectoral made it appear, at first glance, that he'd been hit somewhere in the upper chest.

"My lord, Wild Bill, *what* are you doing on your feet, you brave, foolish thing! Here, lie down on the seat, that's it, just lay your head in my lap. I'll stop the bleeding—Oh, Bill, does it hurt terribly, you brave man?

After her initial shock, Nell now hardly paid any attention to Tate's sprawled body. Her first concern was for Bill's well-being. As she hovered close, her clean, fragrant hair tickling his bare chest, Bill said weakly: "Well, maybe there *is* some pain . . ."

"Of *course* there is, enough to kill a lesser man. Don't play tough for me, poor thing!"

Nell, an avid fan of ladies' romances, now played the heroine to the hilt. She ripped a frilly strip from the bottom of her cotton chemise, baring quite a bit of shapely leg to do so. Lying snugly in her lap, Bill got a firsthand look at that leg. Even better when, as she bent forward to do this, the full weight of her ample bosom smothered Hickok's face in pure pleasure.

Bill lay still, groaning now and then to ratchet up Nell's petting and cooing while she gently wrapped his wound.

"We'll get you to help," Nell fussed, carefully tying the bandage. "Can I do anything else, Bill?"

"Just in case it's—it's curtains for me," Bill managed weakly, "could you . . . I mean, would you consider kissing me? Just an angel's kiss to recommend me to Saint Peter?"

This was a stroke of devious genius. Nell was startled but flattered. Here this handsome man lay, at death's door, gallantly requesting a kiss for the sake of his immortal soul! Even *Jane Eyre* or *The Monk* wasn't this exciting and romantic!

"I'd be absolutely honored," Nell whispered. Slowly her pretty face came lower and closer to Bill's, the heart-shaped lips spreading invitingly for a passionate kiss.

Calamity Jane was gutting a fish on a stump when she heard shots ring out across the ridge. First came the powerful cracks of a rifle, perhaps four or five shots, all close-spaced. These were followed immediately by a string of pistol shots, then an ominous silence.

"Wild Bill!" Jane exclaimed. "That damned litter of prairie rats is after him again!"

Jane gripped her scaling knife and raced toward the crest of the razorback ridge that sheltered her camp. "Any of you bastards kill Bill," she vowed, "I'll hunt you down and cut you from neck to nuts!"

The stage road to Progress City wound around the base of the ridge. Jane immediately spotted the surrey stopped in the road, a well-dressed woman supine on the front seat. A new corpse lay sprawled in the trail. And there was Wild Bill, bleeding a little at the left shoulder but obviously sound as he carefully scanned the terrain for more bushwhackers.

"Them peckerwoods tried to kill you again, purty Bill," Jane said softly. "But the Lord still favors you on account of all my prayers."

Jane's relief, however, quickly turned to a smoldering jealousy as she watched events transpire below. Bill, showing no pain or other sign of serious injury, suddenly turned helpless as the pretty girl revived and began fussing over him.

"Why, that slyboots is playactin' so's she'll drop her linen!"

But Jane's anger did not focus on the young woman. In one of the rare signs of solidarity with other members of the female tribe, Jane seldom blamed Hickok's ladies. Hell's bells, man! How could any woman, even a Carmelite nun, be expected to resist Wild Bill Hickok?

No, damnitall! The transgression was wily Bill's, and his alone. Damn his seductive hide. That poor little gal was no roadhouse whore—why, just *look* at her high-toned refinement! All Bill had to do was be a man and accept his destiny—his *shared* destiny with Jane, which Bill was fighting but would not whip, by the Lord Harry.

The girl's face began to lower closer to Wild Bill's. Jane pulled the Volcanic pistol out of her bright red sash.

"Honey, save that kiss for your mama. *I* got a pill

here for what ails Bill,'' Jane muttered. She thumbed the pistol from half to full cock.

Nell's lips were so close, Bill could feel the heat of them. Just as their flesh was about to meld, one final gunshot split the silence. Wild Bill bucked as if he'd been butt-shot, his hat flying off his head.

This time Nell *did* scream, good and loud. Bill, however, knew damn well who must have made that trick shot—blowing his hat harmlessly off while his head was in a woman's lap!

All of an instant, Bill's ''pain and suffering'' dissipated like smoke in the wind. He sat up quick as a finger snap, hopped nimbly out of the surrey, and retrieved his now-ventillated hat.

''I best be moving on, Nell,'' Bill said hastily.

Nell had not missed this miracle cure. ''I thought you were knocking on Death's door?''

''Nobody home, I reckon,'' Bill replied lamely, trying to sidetrack her with a charming smile.

Nell's dark eyes flashed, then narrowed as indignation swept over her. ''You kill a man, then exploit a woman's shock and emotional turmoil to seduce her in sight of the corpse?''

Bill was already fading back toward the trees where he'd hobbled his roan. ''Tate's past being offended,'' he pointed out. ''And you weren't complaining a few seconds ago about being seduced.''

Nell petulantly stamped one foot. ''I *want* you to seduce me, you gorgeous idiot! But do you have to be so underhanded about it? I want to be taken, not *had*!"

Well Christ, Bill thought in confusion. How can I take you without having you? But he wisely kept that thought to himself, knowing Calamity Jane was impatiently watching his every move.

"Bill? *Bill!* Must you leave now?"

"Two's company, three's a riot!" he shouted back. "I'll see you soon, pretty lady!"

Later that day, cowhands were sent out from the Rocking K to retrieve and bury Barry Tate's body. Tate had been well liked by the Rocking K's hands. There were plenty of somber, angry faces at the special meeting Johnny Kinkaid held that evening in the bunkhouse.

"Boys, there ain't no laurels to be won," Johnny informed them. "But no matter how you slice it, this is a *war*. A buncha left-footed farmers are trying to drive the cattlemen off their own land! And now they've even called in a gun-slick to do their killing for them. Hickok killed Barry in cold blood, that murdering mercenary bastard."

Very few in the group gathered around Johnny knew anything about the secret plan to acquire Turk's Creek for the Burlington. Johnny and Barry had cleverly controlled this "war" so it would appear the farmers were the troublemakers.

The waddie named Danny Ford had been named ramrod in Barry's place. He raised his bandaged right hand. "Hickok blasted my trigger finger off, the bastard! And then he grinned like it was *real* funny.''

''You boys won't have to mix it up with Hickok,'' Johnny promised them. Those cold, stone-gray eyes of his surveyed the group while his right palm rested lightly on the metal backstrap of his big Cavalry pistol. ''Hickok has pushed it to a showdown with me. I want you boys to take care of Dave Hansen and the rest of the hoe-men along Turk's Creek.''

''Take care of 'em how?'' demanded Stoney MacGruder, a big, stupid man with close-spaced eyes.

''You think I want you to powder their butts and tuck 'em in, you muttonhead? *Kill* 'em, for cripe-sakes! Barry ain't taking a nap, you fool, he's dead!''

''We do that,'' Stoney objected, ''won't Hickok have our hides?''

But this time it was Danny Ford, not Johnny, who spoke up. Danny, a veteran of the postbellum Indian Wars, growled at Stoney: ''Damn it, MacGruder, act like you *own* a pair! Didn't Johnny just say *he* would take care of Hickok? How many times you ever seen any man outshoot Johnny Kinkaid? You think he practices hours every day with a short gun so pretti-fied dandies in gold curls can outshoot him?''

Johnny, his handsome features hard as granite in the stark lamplight, nodded gratefully at Danny. Johnny had sent word to Jarvis Blackford about this meeting. But Blackford was noplace to be found. Whatever, Johnny had made up his mind to take no more orders regarding Hickok.

''You boys heard Danny,'' Johnny said. ''Stay frosty and stick together, we'll see this thing through to the roundup. But if we let Hickok keep bluffing and blustering, he'll sink *all* of us faster than you can spit! Once the hoe-men drive out the cattle, *you* boys will either learn how to bale hay or ride back east and get 'factory jobs.' "

This prospect caused a funeral silence throughout the bunkhouse. Nursing beeves was a dirty, rough job. But these weathered bachelors of the plains would rather prod beef for low pay than get rich at a job that took them off their horses.

"We're with you till the wheels fall off, Johnny!" sang out Mace Ludlow. "If any man is faster than Hickok, it's you. You do for him, Johnny. As for the hoe-men, we'll pack them seed-sucking sons a bitches straight to hell!"

Jarvis Blackord, aka Richard Strickland and several other names, had far more in his bag of tricks than false names.

The moment that Blackford learned Hickok had killed Barry Tate, the crafty profiteer realized the death noose was tightening around his own gullet. He packed up his belongings, checked out of his hotel, and retrieved his big claybank from the livery. By the end of that same afternoon, Blackford was well southeast of Progress City. He bore toward the railroad town of Torrington on the Wyoming–Nebraska border. He would set up a new center of operations there.

Blackford had no plans whatsoever to give up this struggle. But from now on, he'd wage a long-distance battle. He knew Bill Hickok was thorough and never overlooked a crime. Even if Blackford could not be linked to any land swindles, he could certainly be linked to Barry Tate. Thus, that meant he could be indicted for conspiracy in the murder of Sheriff Waldo, among other crimes involving Tate.

Which brought Blackford's thoughts back to his literal bag of tricks—his right saddlebag, in which he always carried fresh horseshoes of a different type than the ones on his horse. He also carried the tools needed to reshoe his horse while on the prod.

More than once Blackford had literally established a new trail, soon after a crime, by quickly changing shoes. In case Hickok decided to trail him, Blackford would use the same trick. If necessary, he might even nail the shoes on *backward*. Once before, he had sent a posse tracking north while he fled south.

But even while he gloated over all this, Blackford became gradually aware that his claybank had begun to limp. It was minor, but troubling. Blackford drew rein, swung down, and began inspecting each leg of his horse.

There it was. Left front foreleg. A very tiny crack had worked its way up from the hoof into the coronet, laming the animal. And ironically, it was caused by bad shoeing last time Blackford tried his trick—bad shoeing lamed more horses than any other cause.

Blackford frowned, glancing all around the vast, open country. He felt like a bug inching across a giant soup bowl. He thought again about the rumor circulating back in Progress City: that kill-crazy renegades had jumped the Sioux rez, looking for whiteskin scalps.

He glanced again at that tiny crack. Well, he *should* be all right, he decided, if he didn't have to gallop. He'd nurse the claybank to Torrington, then sell it for glue. And meantime, he'd just hope to hell he didn't have to flee from anyone, or else he was up Salt River.

Chapter Sixteen

Favoring his stiff left shoulder, Wild Bill dipped a hot soda biscuit in the pot liquor from supper.

"Kid," he told Josh, "way you cook? You could hire on with any cattle outfit in the West and *name* your salary. A good cook is worth three top hands."

It was heading on toward sundown. Josh and Wild Bill sat cross-legged before the fire pit in front of the old soddy. Josh could smell the pungent tang of crushed sage, hear the dusty twang of grasshopper wings. But all of it hinted at a peace that wasn't really out there.

The final showdown was coming. Josh figured a man could sense it without being told, like birds sense bad weather.

With his inside eye, Josh saw Sheriff Waldo lying facedown, the back of his head scraped off by a murderous rifle blast. For that crime, among others, Barry Tate was now maggot fodder. And the Kinkaid County War had reached its fever crisis. When that fever finally broke, there would be winners and there would be more dead men.

Bill had fallen into a silent rumination, smoking and staring toward the sawing flames. By old habit, he didn't look directly at the fire for fear of ruining his night vision.

"The *cattlemen* must have poisoned their own cows," Bill muttered, for he had been following this trail of thought for some time now. "That gave them supposed cause to move against the homesteaders. But why on God's green earth would they be so keen to get title to Turk's Creek?"

"Maybe we should talk to the land office clerk again," Josh suggested. "Maybe he—"

"I ain't asking for advice," Bill snapped. "Just thinking out loud."

"Man alive!" Josh exclaimed, tilting the blue-enameled coffeepot to examine the inside in the fire-light.

"What?" Hickok said absently.

"The damned water hereabouts is leaving a ring of crust in this brand-new pot. I can't even scrape it out."

Josh started to set the pot aside. But Wild Bill took it from him and examined it closely in the fading light. He borrowed Josh's pocketknife and scraped at the ring.

"Hard as petrified wood," Bill confirmed. His eyes

met Josh's across the fire pit. "Wonder if all the water around here is like that?"

"I get it!" Josh said excitedly. "You're thinking, if it does *this* to a coffeepot, what's it like in a steam engine?"

Bill nodded. " 'Course, if we're right, that would mean water from Turk's Creek should be different. Maybe you struck a lode after all, Longfellow—maybe I *will* talk to Sam Watson again. Nobody knows details like that better than the land office clerk."

Both men, distracted by this latest conjecture, were abruptly startled by the whinny of an approaching horse. Josh drew his pinfire gun.

"Holster that thumb-buster, you young fool!" Wild Bill admonished him, his hawk eyes squinting to study the gathering twilight. "It's a friendly."

A moment later Nell Kinkaid, wearing a split riding skirt and soft leather boots laced to her knees, rode up on a pretty little calico mare.

"Wild Bill! Thank God I found you. There's more trouble."

Bill helped Nell down from her horse. "There usually is, pretty lady," he remarked, flashing her a smile under his neat mustache. "Me and junior here have got a boxcar full of troubles already. What can you toss in?"

"It's Johnny and the hands. There was a big meeting last night. About what, I can't say. But then today, the men didn't ride out to their usual jobs. They worked on their weapons, shot targets. Some were drinking whiskey in broad daylight despite my father's strict rule about spirits! I don't dare tell father that. Now the men are waiting to ride out later—maybe right about now.''

Bill nodded, rolling all this around in his mind. The fact that Nell had not questioned Bill's killing of Tate proved she understood clear enough what was happening.

''Kid,'' Bill finally told Josh, ''dust your hocks over to Dave Hansen's place. *Pronto*. Tell him to roust out the rest of the hoe-men and wait for me.''

''At Dave's place?''

''No, it won't be safe. Matter fact, tell them all to come here. And kid? Cover your ampersand while you're out there. These half-cocked cowboys will be kill-crazy.''

Josh nodded and whistled for his little blue, starting to rig him. While Josh tightened cinches and tested latigos, he hid on the Indian side of his horse, out of sight as he listened to more of the conversation.

''Bill, all this lately is practically killing my father! He knows—well, he *suspects* that my brother is about to challenge you. Johnny always practices shooting, but he's been relentless about it these past few days. Eight, even ten hours of nonstop practice. Bill, he's . . . frighteningly adept with a gun.''

Bill laughed at her choice of words. '' 'Adept'? I've seen him shoot, dumpling. He's one of those rare men who aims with his instincts, not his eyes, and I've never seen a man who can clear a gun from a holster that quick.''

"Are you listening to yourself?" Nell said, her tone miserable. "You just described Bill Hickok, too! Father is absolutely terrified about losing Johnny. If Johnny's killed, so is the Kinkaid line of descent. Besides that, bad or not, he's my brother, and I love him. But if *you're* killed . . ."

Nell trailed off, her voice desperate as she made it clear: Either way, as she and Elmer both saw it, there could be no "winners" in a gunfight between Johnny and Wild Bill.

"Bill? You have to try and understand about my brother. It's *not* that he's a good man. He's not. Johnny doesn't care at all what kind of low, mean things his companions do, he'll drink with them."

"Murder included?"

She swallowed, then nodded. "Murder included, I'm afraid. But . . . I think his Kinkaid pride keeps him from sinking quite to their level. I've never seen such goings-on among supposed Christians as we have around here lately. But I honestly believe Johnny *himself* has drawn the line at murder."

"Those who hold a candle for the devil," Bill told her, "are doing the devil's work."

By now Josh's *grullo* was saddled. But he lingered in the shadows on the far side for a few moments, watching Nell step into Bill's arms.

"You bolted to the ground, Longfellow?" Bill demanded without even turning his head. "Take my message to Hansen. Every second counts now."

But *you'll* have time to "comfort" Nell after I leave, Josh thought resentfully. Nonetheless, he stepped up into leather and kicked his pony into motion.

About an hour and a half later, they met right behind the soddy in a moonlit meadow that had been grazed to stubble: Wild Bill Hickok, Dave Hansen, Lonnie Peatross, and a dozen other beleaguered farmers from the Turk Creek area.

"Let's look truth straight in the eye, boys," Wild Bill exhorted them. "The cowmen will strike this very night in force. What they *want* is to catch each of you at home alone."

"Like they done to Dave's cousin," spoke up a man with wind-cracked lips in a thin, sharp-nosed face. Josh recognized the rifle under his arm as a Winchester .44-90.

"I know cowboys like most men know their wife's geography," Bill went on. "I was a cowtown starman. Cowboys're tough at what they do, all right. But off the job, most of 'em are just hell-raisers, not killers. All holler and no heart. Sure, they like to toss lead. But very few of 'em got the stomach for a hard fight. So you're going to fort up and *give* them a hard fight, if they want one."

"Fort up?" Lonnie demanded. "Here, you mean?"

Bill shook his head. "This is open country, and that's good. But *open* isn't enough. Remember: Before they give up, they're going to push hard just to see if you move. It's got beyond fence-cutting and crop-trampling. So besides open country, *take the high ground.* Throw up a fortress. Store water, plenty of ammo, and bandage cloth.''

Bill nodded toward a distant pocket of cattle grazing the far side of the meadow. ''Kill some butcher beef, too. They've called you rustlers, shot you for rustlers, might as well put the deed to the word.''

Josh realized no one was asking what Wild Bill had in mind for his own share in this looming battle. By now, the word was all over the county that Johnny Kinkaid was spoiling for a showdown with Hickok.

''Listen!'' Dave Hansen called out. ''Riders! Passing south of us.''

''That'll be our brave ranger force from the Rocking K,'' Bill said sarcastically. ''No doubt looking to catch their first farmer. You boys know what to do. I suggest you hump it.''

After the sodbusters rode out to establish their bastion, Wild Bill and Josh were left to wait out an uneasy night.

At first, they took two-hour turns sleeping and standing ''fire watch,'' as Bill called it. But as the activity of night riders increased all around them, both men finally gave up any attempt at sleeping.

They heard plenty of shooting, occasional shouts and whistles, the thudding drumbeat of hooves as the marauding cowboys pounded their mounts across the county, raising hell.

Toward dawn, Josh watched Bill carefully wiping out the bores of his Peacemakers with clean patches. Josh knew, both from study and firsthand observation, how Hickok operated. Once the man was sure he was plagued by a boil, his immediate reaction was to lance it.

"You're going to call him out after sunup, are'n'cha?" Josh demanded. "Johnny Kinkaid, I mean?"

"No," Bill said matter-of-factly. "*You* are."

Josh felt his jaw drop open. "Me? Bill, I can hit a target pretty good, but—"

Wild Bill snorted at the kid's misunderstanding. "No, you young idiot. After breakfast you're going to take him a note from me. It'll tell Kinkaid where to meet me. I'm damned if we'll burn powder in front of Elmer and Nell."

"I'll take the note," Josh agreed. "But I'm coming to the fight too, Bill. And this time I *ain't* asking you, I don't care how famous you are. This is news, Wild Bill, history, and I got a right—why, a *duty*—to tell it."

Bill dismissed all this with a wave of one disassembled pistol.

"Kid, just shit-can the highfalutin rhetoric, wouldja? Go where you want, I ain't your mother. But speaking of her: If you get in the way and get yourself killed, don't expect *me* to write to your ma about it."

This prospect was so hilarious (Josh's prim-and-proper Quaker mother receiving a missive from the most notorious gunfighter in the West!) that Josh laughed outright, and so did Bill. But seconds later, another explosion of cracking gunfire over the next ridge sobered their faces.

Chapter Seventeen

Much later that day, when it was finally over, Josh would describe the showdown in a wire story that became as widely read throughout America as the *Holy Bible* or *Leslie's Weekly.*

Josh had delivered the "summons" from Wild Bill without alerting Elmer or Nell, both of whom were evidently still asleep when Josh arrived just past sunup at the Rocking K. He pushed the note for Johnny into the sleepy maid's hand, telling her to deliver it immediately. Then the nervous reporter hightailed it for the rendezvous point mentioned in Bill's note: the deserted line shack on the north boundary of Elmer's land.

It was a good spot, Josh realized now as he tied his horse out of harm's way behind the shack, next to Bill's roan. A big, level clearing in front of the shack was surrounded by a buffer of thick ponderosa pine—no one back at the main yard would even hear the shots.

Not that such discretion mattered much now. For only a mile north of here, a pitched battle had begun just past dawn. The rover force of marauding cowboys had finally discovered the high-ground fort thrown up by the hoe-men. A hammering racket of gunshots split what should have been a peaceful morning stillness.

"The farmers will hold," Bill said with quiet confidence. He stood out in the center of the big clearing. But with his usual caution, he had placed his back to the bole of a tree that had escaped cutting. Now he stood facing the only approach to the line shack, enjoying the day's first cheroot. Bill's fathomless eyes watched drifting pockets of morning mist.

Josh searched Bill's face for signs of fear but found nothing, not a damn thing at all. *The truth be told*, he would write only a few hours from now, *Bill Hickok does indeed kill in cold blood. But it's not the cold blood of a criminal without honor—it's the utter indifference of an eagle destroying its prey from instinct.*

"The farmers will hold," Bill repeated, flicking off a gray pellet of ash from his cigar. "They whipped a damn tough army of Mexican regulars in '47 and they were the best soldiers on *both* sides in the Great War. They'll hang on like ticks."

"Listen! Somebody's coming!" Josh said suddenly.

Bill nodded, carefully butting his half-smoked cheroot and slipping it back into the pocket of his leather vest.

"That'll be Johnny Kinkaid," he said. "Get inside the shack, kid. You can see your big story from the doorway."

Josh, who had learned from Bill to give as good as he got, shot back: "What if Kinkaid *kills* you, Bill? Don'tcha want to scratch out a will, at least tell me where to send your belongings?"

Bill's strong white teeth flashed in a grin. "They say a man is usually killed by what he loves most. So I figure I'll die at a poker table someday. But kid? *You* best hope I ain't plugged today. 'Cause if I am? That means Calamity Jane will have only *you* to comfort her."

Josh felt his face draining white. Seeing this, Bill laughed so hard he made himself cough. "Now scram, Longfellow! Here comes our man."

Josh was safe inside the shack by the time Johnny entered the big clearing. He spotted Hickok waiting and drew rein, swinging deftly down from the saddle. Kinkaid moved his dun out of the line of fire and ground-hitched him. So far, he'd said nothing to Hickok. It was Wild Bill who spoke first.

"Morning, Johnny," he called out. "Tell me something, wouldja? How come you been so afraid to meet me? The whole time I've been in these parts, you've taken pains to avoid me. Even now you won't meet my eye. You afraid to kill a man you know?"

"I'll be looking right at you in just a few shakes," Johnny promised.

Josh watched the handsome young tough swagger out toward the center of the clearing, his face twisted with insolence. The Smith & Wesson pistol tied low in its hand-tooled holster seemed huge—even longer and heavier than Bill's Peacemakers. Even from the shack, Josh could see that Johnny had filed the notch off his hammer so it wouldn't snag coming out of the holster.

"Hell," Bill said amiably, "*I* killed one of my own best friends once, deliberately. Also shot my favorite deputy, though *that* one was a sloppy accident. Got me fired."

Josh knew both claims were straight. When Bill found out a fellow Union scout was actually a Rebel, he gunned him down without mercy or debate. The deputy incident was more embarrassing—Bill got his targets mixed up in a heated, confused gun battle.

"The hell *I* care, Hickok?" Johnny retorted. "Quit flapping your gums, dandy man, and make your play."

"Yep," Bill said, pushing away from the tree, "I'd just as soon know who I'm killing. But that's me, I guess. Now, of course, a fellow who was really a coward at heart might feel different."

"Whack the cork, Hickok, goddamn you to hell! I said just make your play!"

"Yep, a man who shoots *targets* all the livelong day," Bill went on, "can shape himself into a damn good marksman. But you know what, Johnny? He can't make himself into a *killer* that way. You, Kinkaid, are a target shooter, not a gunfighter."

By now Johnny was red-faced with rage. But Josh read something else in those twisted features: The man was *scared.* His left hand trembled so violently, he had to grip his thigh to steady it. Lord God, Josh thought, I bet Custer's smug face looked like that a minute before he went under.

"God*damn* you, Hickok! I said *draw*!"

"Yes indeed," Bill continued to goad. "I had my suspicions about you. The mountain men called it buck ager. Sort of a womanish weakness that washes over some men when it comes time to kill."

That last barb struck deep and evoked a snarl of rage from the conceited Johnny. His gun hand moved so quick that Josh would have missed even the blur of it if he had blinked. But incredibly, Bill's Colt barked first—two rapid shots back to back. And for the first—and only—time in his life during a showdown, Wild Bill Hickok aimed to maim, not kill.

Later, when his turbulent emotions calmed, Josh figured it all out. Bill did it for Nell and Elmer. With ruthless precision, Hickok deliberately destroyed Johnny's gun hand for life. Two bullets shattered the delicate and intricate hand and finger bones beyond healing. Kinkaid would be lucky to ever hold a coffee mug again with that hand, let alone master a gun.

Johnny's gun had flown from his hand. Josh expected him to try picking it up and firing it with his left hand. But Kinkaid, wracked by intense pain, was already going into shock. He simply sat upon the ground like a half-wit, staring at his mangled, bleeding hand from glazed eyes like glass orbs. He looked so pathetic and lost that Josh couldn't even hate him, though he knew he should.

Quickly, the two companions wrapped the wounded hand in a bandanna and lifted a now docile Kinkaid into the saddle. Bill whacked the horse's rump, and by habit it began trotting back to its stall at the ranch.

"Let's go see about the rest of your story, kid," Bill said, retrieving his own horse. "They're still busting caps at Fort Farmer."

But Bill's prediction proved right as rain.

The cowboy aggressors had shown much enthusiasm for a fight when it was just noise and bravado. Once a few of them were blown out of their saddles, however, the rest lost their fighting fettle.

By the time Josh and Wild Bill reached the high-ground fortress of sod and stones, the cattlemen had fled—leaving Danny Ford, Mace Ludlow, and a third corpse behind on the slope.

Late that afternoon, back in the hotel now, some more welcome news reached Wild Bill and Josh. Jarvis Blackford's horse had evidently gone lame on the road to Torrington. Thus handicapped, he had the misfortune of crossing paths with those Sioux renegades who jumped the rez. His remains were found buried up to the neck on the open prairie. The eyelids had been sliced clean off so the sun would slowly dry up the eyeballs while ants bit at them.

"Musta been a mite unpleasant" was Bill's only comment when he heard about it. And Josh used that very line to end his remarkable dispatch.

With Blackford thus removed, the scheme to steal Turk's Creek just dried up like milkweeds in the sun. The farmers ended up striking a lucrative deal with the Burlington for water rights.

His job done, Wild Bill Hickok again harked to the lure of Denver's many faro games and roulette wheels. But Josh soon realized Bill had one last bit of unfinished business—or rather, pleasure. Her name was Nell Kinkaid.

However, as a frustrated Wild Bill would explain later, their pleasurable interlude turned into a disaster.

Nell had invited Wild Bill to the county fair in Evansville. Bill had somehow made a quiet arrangement with a hotel clerk there—not only was this town twenty miles from Progress City, but its residents were gone anyway, visiting the nearby fair. Bill had no trouble whatsoever slipping a veiled Nell Kinkaid into the room for a day's pleasure.

But he had foolishly underrated Calamity Jane's vigilance. Bill had *just* gotten Nell between satin sheets when the bed collapsed with a resounding crash. Even worse, a huge and harmless—but extremely ugly—gopher snake slithered over Nell and Bill's naked flesh as it escaped from the bed where Jane had planted it earlier. To cap all that, Bill reported morosely, Jane shot the window out and screamed at the top of her lungs, "Cowards to the rear!"

Needless to report, Bill's amorous ambitions were soundly thwarted yet again. The incident left him in such a foul mood, he didn't even confess any of this until he and Josh were halfway back to Denver. But the humor of it finally caught up with Bill. Both men stopped in the middle of the trail and laughed until tears streamed from their eyes.

"That woman is so ugly," Bill said when he could speak again, "you could throw her in a lake and skim ugly for a month. But she does keep life interesting, kid, I'll give her that. C'mon, Longfellow, let's make tracks. There's two steak dinners in Denver, with all the trimmings, and damned if they ain't got our names on 'em."

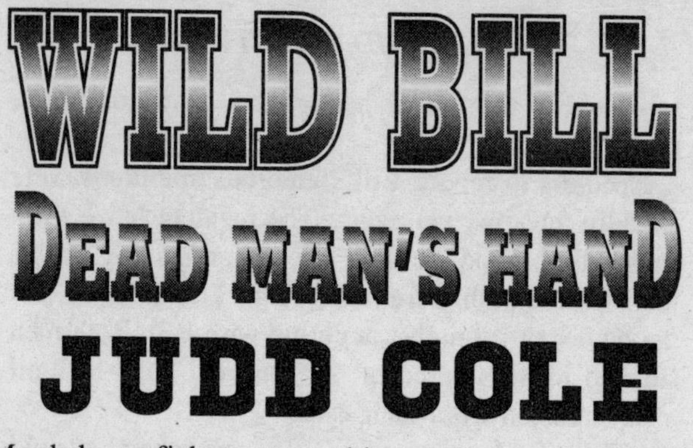

Marshal, gunfighter, stage driver, and scout, Wild Bill Hickok has a legend as big and untamed as the West itself. No man is as good with a gun as Wild Bill, and few men use one as often. From Abilene to Deadwood, his name is known by all—and feared by many. That's why he is hired by Allan Pinkerton's new detective agency to protect an eccentric inventor on a train ride through the worst badlands of the West. With hired thugs out to kill him and angry Sioux out for his scalp, Bill knows he has his work cut out for him. But even if he survives that, he has a still worse danger to face—a jealous Calamity Jane.

___4487-0 $3.99 US/$4.99 CAN

Dorchester Publishing Co., Inc.
P.O. Box 6640
Wayne, PA 19087-8640

Please add $1.75 for shipping and handling for the first book and $.50 for each book thereafter. NY, NYC, and PA residents, please add appropriate sales tax. No cash, stamps, or C.O.D.s. All orders shipped within 6 weeks via postal service book rate.
Canadian orders require $2.00 extra postage and must be paid in U.S. dollars through a U.S. banking facility.

Name____
Address____
City______________________State________Zip________
I have enclosed $__________ in payment for the checked book(s).
Payment must accompany all orders. ☐ Please send a free catalog.
CHECK OUT OUR WEBSITE! www.dorchesterpub.com

DAN'L BOONE

DODGE TYLER

THE KAINTUCKS

The Natchez Trace is the trail of choice for frontiersmen heading north from New Orleans. But for Dan'l Boone and his small band of boatmen, the trail leads straight into danger. Lying in wait for the legendary guide is a band of French land pirates out for the payroll he is protecting. And with the cutthroats is a vicious war party of Chickasaw braves out for much more—Dan'l Boone's blood!

4466-8 $3.99 US/$4.99 CAN

Dorchester Publishing Co., Inc.
P.O. Box 6640
Wayne, PA 19087-8640

Please add $1.75 for shipping and handling for the first book and $.50 for each book thereafter. NY, NYC, and PA residents, please add appropriate sales tax. No cash, stamps, or C.O.D.s. All orders shipped within 6 weeks via postal service book rate.
Canadian orders require $2.00 extra postage and must be paid in U.S. dollars through a U.S. banking facility.

Name__________________________________
Address________________________________
City__________________State______Zip________
I have enclosed $________ in payment for the checked book(s).
Payment must accompany all orders. ☐ Please send a free catalog.

DAN'L BOONE

WARRIOR'S TRACE

Dodge Tyler

The Kentucky River has long been the lifeblood of American settlers near Dan'l Boone's home of Boonesborough. But suddenly it is running red with blood of another kind. The Shawnee and the Fox tribe have joined together in an unprecedented war to drive the white man out of their lands once and for all. And if Dan'l can't whip the desperate settlers into a mighty fighting force soon, he—and all of Boonesborough—might not survive the next attack.

___4421-8 $3.99 US/$4.99 CAN

Dorchester Publishing Co., Inc.
P.O. Box 6640
Wayne, PA 19087-8640

Please add $1.75 for shipping and handling for the first book and $.50 for each book thereafter. NY, NYC, and PA residents, please add appropriate sales tax. No cash, stamps, or C.O.D.s. All orders shipped within 6 weeks via postal service book rate.
Canadian orders require $2.00 extra postage and must be paid in U.S. dollars through a U.S. banking facility.

Name____
Address______________________________________
City____________________State______Zip__________
I have enclosed $__________ in payment for the checked book(s).
Payment must accompany all orders. ❑ Please send a free catalog.
CHECK OUT OUR WEBSITE! www.dorchesterpub.com

David Thompson

With only his oldest friend and his trusty long rifle for company, Davy Crockett explores the wild frontier looking for adventure, and has the strength and cunning to face any enemy. But even he may have met his match when he gets caught between two warring tribes on one side and a dangerous band of white men on the other—all of them willing to die—and kill—for a group of stolen women. It is up to Crockett to save the women, his friend and his own hide if he wants to live to explore another day.

_4229-0 $3.99 US/$4.99 CAN

Dorchester Publishing Co., Inc.
P.O. Box 6640
Wayne, PA 19087-8640

Please add $1.75 for shipping and handling for the first book and $.50 for each book thereafter. NY, NYC, and PA residents, please add appropriate sales tax. No cash, stamps, or C.O.D.s. All orders shipped within 6 weeks via postal service book rate.
Canadian orders require $2.00 extra postage and must be paid in U.S. dollars through a U.S. banking facility.

Name_______________________________________
Address_____________________________________
City_____________________State_______Zip________
I have enclosed $__________ in payment for the checked book(s).
Payment must accompany all orders. ❑ Please send a free catalog.

Davy Crockett is driven by a powerful need to explore, to see what lies beyond the next hill. On a trip through the swamp country along the Gulf of Mexico, Davy and his old friend Flavius meet up for the first time with Jim Bowie, a man who will soon become a legend of the West—and who is destined to play an important part in Davy's dramatic life. Neither Davy nor Jim know the meaning of the word "surrender," and when they run afoul of a deadly tribe of cannibals, they know it will be a fight to the death.

___4443-9 $3.99 US/$4.99 CAN

Dorchester Publishing Co., Inc.
P.O. Box 6640
Wayne, PA 19087-8640

Please add $1.75 for shipping and handling for the first book and $.50 for each book thereafter. NY, NYC, and PA residents, please add appropriate sales tax. No cash, stamps, or C.O.D.s. All orders shipped within 6 weeks via postal service book rate.
Canadian orders require $2.00 extra postage and must be paid in U.S. dollars through a U.S. banking facility.

Name______________________________
Address______________________________
City______________________State________Zip____________
I have enclosed $__________ in payment for the checked book(s).
Payment must accompany all orders. ❑ Please send a free catalog.
CHECK OUT OUR WEBSITE! www.dorchesterpub.com

DAVY CROCKETT

HOMECOMING

DAVID THOMPSON

Davy Crockett lives for adventure. With a faithful friend at his side and a trusty long rifle in his hand, the fearless frontiersman sets out for the Great Lakes territories. But the region surrounding the majestic inland seas is full of Indians both peaceful and bloodthirsty. And when the brave pioneer saves a Chippewa maiden from warriors of a rival tribe, his travels become a deadly struggle to save his scalp. If Crockett can't defeat his fierce foes, the only remains he'll leave will be his legend and his coonskin cap.

___4112-X $3.99 US/$4.99 CAN

Dorchester Publishing Co., Inc.
P.O. Box 6640
Wayne, PA 19087-8640

Please add $1.75 for shipping and handling for the first book and $.50 for each book thereafter. NY, NYC, and PA residents, please add appropriate sales tax. No cash, stamps, or C.O.D.s. All orders shipped within 6 weeks via postal service book rate.
Canadian orders require $2.00 extra postage and must be paid in U.S. dollars through a U.S. banking facility.

Name____
Address____
City__________________________State________Zip__________
I have enclosed $__________ in payment for the checked book(s).
Payment must accompany all orders. ❑ Please send a free catalog.

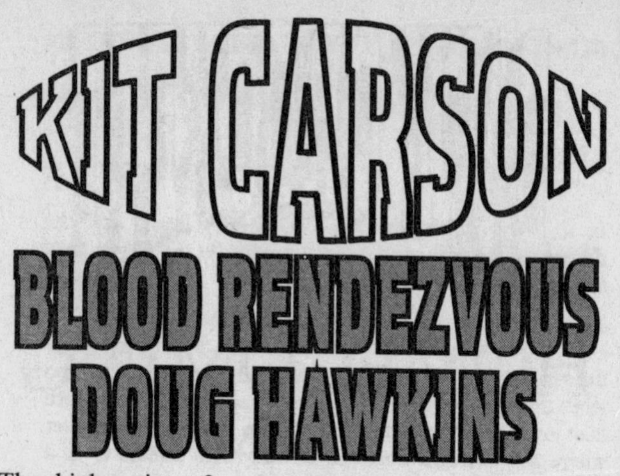

The high point of any trapper's year is the summer rendezvous, the annual gathering where mountain men from all over the frontier meet to trade the pelts they risked their lives for. But for Kit Carson, the real danger lies in getting to the rendezvous. He is leading a party of trappers, all of them weighed down with a year's worth of furs. That is enough to make them a tempting target for any killer on the trail—especially when the trail leads through Blackfoot territory.

__4499-4 $3.99 US/$4.99 CAN

Dorchester Publishing Co., Inc.
P.O. Box 6640
Wayne, PA 19087-8640

Please add $1.75 for shipping and handling for the first book and $.50 for each book thereafter. NY, NYC, and PA residents, please add appropriate sales tax. No cash, stamps, or C.O.D.s. All orders shipped within 6 weeks via postal service book rate.
Canadian orders require $2.00 extra postage and must be paid in U.S. dollars through a U.S. banking facility.

Name____
Address____
City________________________State________Zip__________
I have enclosed $__________ in payment for the checked book(s).
Payment must accompany all orders. ❑ Please send a free catalog.
CHECK OUT OUR WEBSITE! www.dorchesterpub.com

In the days of the musket, the powder horn, and the flintlock, one pioneer ventures forth into the virgin land that will become the United States.

#5: Apache Revenge. A band of Apaches with blood in their eyes ride the warpath right to Dan'l's door, looking to avenge their humiliating defeat at his hands three years earlier. And when they capture Dan'l's niece as a trophy it becomes more than just a battle for Dan'l, it becomes personal. No matter where the warriors ride, the frontiersman swears to find them, to get the girl back—and to exact some vengeance of his own.

_4183-9 $4.99 US/$5.99 CAN

#4: Winter Kill. Gold fever—the treacherous disease caused the vicious ends of many pioneers. One winter, Dan'l finds himself making a dangerous trek for lost riches buried in lands held sacred by the Sioux. Soon, Boone is fighting with all his skill and cunning to win a battle against hostile Sioux warriors, ferocious animals, and a blizzard that would bury a lesser man in a horrifying avalanche of death.

_4087-5 $4.99 US/$5.99 CAN

Dorchester Publishing Co., Inc.
P.O. Box 6640
Wayne, PA 19087-8640

Please add $1.75 for shipping and handling for the first book and $.50 for each book thereafter. NY, NYC, and PA residents, please add appropriate sales tax. No cash, stamps, or C.O.D.s. All orders shipped within 6 weeks via postal service book rate. Canadian orders require $2.00 extra postage and must be paid in U.S. dollars through a U.S. banking facility.

Name______________________________________
Address____________________________________
City_____________________ State________ Zip__________
I have enclosed $__________ in payment for the checked book(s).
Payment must accompany all orders. ☐ Please send a free catalog.

SPECIAL
TOLL-FREE NUMBER

1-800-481-9191

Call Monday through Friday
10 a.m. to 9 p.m.
Eastern Time
Get a free catalogue,
join the Western Book Club,
and order books using your
Visa, MasterCard,
or Discover®.

Leisure
Books

GO ONLINE WITH US AT DORCHESTERPUB.COM